Timeless T:

COPYRIGHT © 2024

Edited by James Hancock & Kerr Pelto

Foreword by Kerr Pelto

All rights reserved. No reproduction without the prior permission of the authors.

FIRST EDITION

This book is a work of fiction. Names, characters, and incidents are products of the author's imagination, and any resemblance to actual events or persons, living or dead, is entirely coincidental.

Thanks to all the unsung heroes – Family & Friends
across the world, who are forced to endure first drafts.

Contents

Foreword	1
On the Road to Ensenada By Robert Burns	3
Cookie By James Hancock	5
Type Specimen By Séimí Mac Aindreasa	11
A Stab in the Dark By Kerr Pelto	17
The Grind By Bryn Eliesse	21
The Hell Gate Gambit By Ryan Fleming	27
Ingredients of a Life Not Worth Living By Teodora Vamvu	33
Glimmers Of Life By Sarah Turner	37

Shoe Snob 43
By Mikayla Hill

Jack 47
By Oluseyi Onabanjo

Lucky Penny 53
By James Hancock

Drizzle 59
By Robert Burns

Find Love Here 61
By Kerr Pelto

Acidity 65
By Bryn Eliesse

A Death Celebrated 69
By Séimí Mac Aindreasa

Bad Water 75
By Ryan Fleming

Honour 79
By James Hancock

Swan Song in G Minor 81
By Robert Burns

Carl 83
By Sarah Turner

Jàpà 89
By Oluseyi Onabanjo

Kiss of Death 93
By Teodora Vamvu

Unicorn 97
By Mikayla Hill

Last Straw 99
By James Hancock

The Lighthouse 103
By Kerr Pelto

Estate Sale 107
By Bryn Eliesse

Stamp Collector 111
By Robert Burns

Sub-Paranormal Activities 115
By Séimí Mac Aindreasa

Bittersweet 121
By Ryan Fleming

Brute 127
By Sarah Turner

Shelf Life 131
By James Hancock

A Taste of Indulgence 135
By Bryn Eliesse

Kpalongo 141
By Oluseyi Onabanjo

The Regular 147
By Robert Burns

The Story of Us 151
By Teodora Vamvu

Raincoat and Tissues 155
By Kerr Pelto

Foreword

When I was asked to join another anthology following our *Bring Out the Wicked* book published on Amazon, I was thrilled to once again collaborate with writers I have grown to admire. It has been my great privilege to be selected to write with them, exchange stories, and harness the creativity of their minds to make my stories better.

There's something satisfying to the soul, seeing your name in print. To hold a book in your hand and thumb through the pages to your short stories, read them, sigh with gratitude, then snuggle the book between favorite authors on the shelf.

All stories in this book are flash fiction, under 1,000 words, and can be read quickly. Let these stories take you out of your daily grind and into the minds of ten writers from around the world. Each author has their own flair, their own style of putting the puzzle pieces of a story together. Let us fill you with fantasy, give you a laugh, possibly make you grimace, and maybe shed a tear.

So, go ahead, turn the page and be prepared to find love, enjoy unexpected twists, and have goosebumps crawl up your arms. But don't worry, they're all fiction.

Well, maybe not all.

Kerr Pelto

On the Road to Ensenada

Robert Burns

The barren road approaching Ensenada from the north is never very busy, especially this late at night. Highway 3 meanders in a broken line through arid sagebrush as it cleaves the vast Pacific Ocean on the one side from the Sierra de Juarez range on the other.

I like this part of the journey. On most runs, I can be alone for a while, racing through Baja in my Chevy Super 8. Tonight is different, though. Tonight, I'm not alone.

I roll the windows down and turn the radio up. The salty winds blowing off the ocean dance with the mariachi music and sober me as we float through the sultry, narcotic Mexican night.

Halfway across the midnight expanse, we pull over for a few minutes, and I climb out of the roadster. Leaning against the chrome of the front bumper, I light up a cigarette and embrace the darkness that blankets me.

The swollen moon begins its pass behind a cloud, dripping an inky blue shadow onto my white linen shirt. I watch the velvet sky expand in all directions with an infinite blackness, punctuated by the sharp pinpoints of a billion glittering white stars. The ash of the cigarette brightens as I take a drag, its warmth caressing my face with a vermilion glow.

I picture the end of the road: the vast brown desert floor behind us exchanged for the infinite blue of the Pacific ahead.

"You always loved the ocean," I tell Phoebe. "The blue matches your eyes."

I settle back behind the wheel and gun the engine as we pull away from the shoulder and take off again, returning to the broken blacktop. The moon rejoins us for this last part of our pilgrimage, reclaiming its place among the stars.

We top the hill and prepare for our descent into the sleepy village, the twinkle of its pre-dawn lights coming into view ahead, fishing boats bobbing dockside. I cut the radio off, and the Chevy flies on in silence.

"We're almost there," I say to Phoebe, as I stroke the urn that cradles her, safe and secure in the passenger seat.

The sanguine dawn crests the mountains opposite the sea, and the sun pokes a sleepy eye over the ridge. Sensing its certain defeat, the moon bids farewell and sends us on our way south to where Phoebe will finally rest.

Cookie

James Hancock

I've read stories of people finding the face of Jesus in strange places: burnt onto a piece of toast, stained onto a mattress, or shaped amongst a formation of rocks. Idiots trying to get their name in the paper. Attention seekers. I always considered it something not worth considering, until I found my face on a cookie. One of twelve homemade cookies, and there I was, in all my side profile glory.

Time seemed to move slowly as my eyes adjusted and brain reacted. I stood vulnerable, alone in my kitchen, wearing nothing but pants and staring at a perfectly formed likeness of myself. I shrieked out loud.

My wife came running. "What is it? Are you ok?"

Wide-eyed and giddy with shock, I turned to face her and held up the cookie.

"Oat and raisin. Your favourite."

Could she not see it? See me? It was blatant. I turned my head side on and held the cookie close. I frowned and pouted to match the cookie's expression.

"Are you ok, Terry? You've gone a bit pale."

"I'm on the cookie!" I stared her in the eyes and spoke slowly, yet forcefully. "It's a sign, Sharon. A sign!"

She leaned close and squinted, trying to see what I could. "What am I looking at?"

I pointed. She concentrated. I dropped my arms by my side and sighed. It was a waste of time, she couldn't see it. I placed the cookie next to the others on the cooling rack. "Don't eat it. I'm phoning the local newspaper."

She smiled, waiting for the punchline, but quickly realised there was no joke. "Are you serious? You can't..."

I placed a finger on her lips, cutting her sentence short. "This is big," I whispered. "We're going to be rich, Sharon. Famous!" I withdrew my finger and held it up to 'mark my words'.

"You're nuts." Sharon's smile dropped. She shook her head and walked out of the kitchen. "Nuts!" Her remark was quickly followed by thumping up the stairs, purposefully drowning out any last word attempt on my part.

I turned my attention back to the cookie. There was something different. Was there something different? I leaned in close to take a better look. Yes, my face was smiling. A definite smile where a straight mouth had been before.

"What's going on?" I whispered to the cookie. "What are you?"

The mouth moved. "Eat me, Terry!" The voice was quiet and husky, yet carried a persuasive tone. "Eat me!"

Startled, I stepped back and put my hand to my mouth, stopping myself from crying out. How was this possible? Was it really happening, or was I losing my mind? Oh God! I was losing my mind!

"You talked," I said, stating the obvious, but I needed to hear myself say it.

"Eat me, Terry." Its raisin eye turned slightly, looking right at me.

"What?" The question came from my mouth, even though I was thinking, 'how', 'why', and 'have I gone insane?' This was as far from 'normal' as things got.

"Eat me!" it spoke again. "Eat me... or I'll eat you!"

I snapped my gawping mouth shut. The room filled with a silent chill as the cookie stretched a foreboding grin. If I was a victim of my own cookie-related insanity, I had just threatened myself. And if I was perfectly sane, then a cookie had just threatened me. Either way, the strangeness of the morning had just cranked up several notches.

"Are you threatening me?" I looked at the cookie sternly and found my inner-authoritarian voice. "I don't take kindly to being threatened."

"What ya gonna do about it, fat boy?" the cookie replied.

"Fat boy?" I said, huffing as I searched for a quick comeback. "I don't take kindly to being insulted either..." The cookie interrupted with a fake crying sound and a mocking whine.

"Oh, boo hoo. Did I hurt little baby's feelings? Maybe I should have said, fat girl!"

"FAT GIRL!" I snapped, thumping my fist down on top of the cookie and obliterating it.

I lifted my crumb-coated hand and looked at the scattered remains, tears welling in my eyes as I realised what I had done. I was gone; destroyed by my own rage.

"I'm not a girl." I wept and shoved a handful of cookie pieces into my mouth. I chewed fast and angrily, sobbing as I did. I chomped and bawled, raining tears and crumbs onto the kitchen floor, and smearing sticky fingers across my face.

"Why? Why did you make me do..."

"You ok, Terry?" Sharon spoke softly from the kitchen doorway.

I shook my head pathetically and sniffed back the tears. "No," I muttered quietly and reached out open arms. She hugged me. I needed a hug. I clearly needed several other things too. A few more hours sleep, a holiday, and potentially a psychiatrist. But most of all, I needed a glass of milk. That cookie was dry!

I'd been working long hours, and the early mornings had taken their toll. The cookie was broken, but hopefully, I wasn't.

Concerned by my meltdown, Sharon held me in her arms and gently shushed me whilst rubbing my back. "There, there, it's okay." Glancing at the remaining cookies, she could have sworn one of them looked strangely familiar. Yes, a clear resemblance to her late mother.

And... hold on... was it smiling?

Type Specimen

Séimí Mac Aindreasa

The weather without may have been inclement, but it was as nothing to the storm brewing within the darkened interior of Maddens Bar. Therein, topics of earth-shattering importance were being discussed.

"So, why do ye think they'd pick you?" asked Rory, tilting a pint of Guinness back to catch the last drops.

Paff laughed, a sly look in his eyes. "Cos, nobody else has applied for the job. Not for ages anyway."

Gerry cocked an inquiring head at Paff. "Why not? Ye'd think there'd be people queuin' up for a job like that!"

Paff laughed. "That's what I thought too. But apparently the last fella to apply was like, a hundred years ago or something. So, I reckon I'm in with a shout."

Seamus paused mid-swallow of his pint. "Sorry, but what the fuck are ye talkin' about? What job? Sure, Paff hasn't had a job in years! What are youse on about?"

Rory, reaching for his next drink, rolled his eyes. "Paff here wants to be a typical spaceman, or something."

Paff spluttered, sending droplets of phlegm and Porter across the table. The others instinctively sat back and covered their glasses.

"It's called the Type Specimen, dickhead! I'm gonna apply to have me skeleton kept as the Type Specimen!"

"Oh aye?" Seamus said, a hint of mockery in his voice. "And what's that, when it's at home?"

Paff sputtered anew, eliciting more back-sitting and pint-covering. "Jesus friggin' Christ! I've just spent the last ten minutes explainin' it to ye!"

"Ach, sure I tuned out when the race started. What was it again?" Seamus winked at the others. Craic and banter were afoot.

Paff's dander was up. For someone who could spy a free drink from across a crowded bar, he always failed to spot the urine being extracted from him right in front of his eyes.

"Fer God's sake! The Type Specimen is the skeleton for the human race! It's the skeleton that people look at and think – aye, that's the human skeleton!"

Rory paused in his drinking and shot Paff a confused look.

"Sure, wouldn't they do that if they looked at any skeleton?"

"Yes, but the actual one – the official one – would be mine! I'd be famous!"

Rory put down the pint and fixed an inquisitive eye on his compadre. "You'd be dead, though. Well, ye'd have to be, wouldn't ye? Unless – do they X-ray ye?"

"Whaddya mean, do they X-ray ye?" Paff exclaimed.

Gerry, barely hiding a grin, picked up the baton. "Like, do they just bring ye in and give ye like, a full-body X-ray and then that's it? They just say – aye, here it is; the type whatever for the whole human race?"

Paff's eyes almost rolled into the back of his head at this apparent lack of intelligence. "Of course not! What are ye talkin' about? They display your skeleton in a case! It's meant to represent the pinnacle of the human race! They don't show your skeleton until yer dead! They – I don't know – they remove yer skeleton before ye get buried, clean it, and then put it in a case or something!"

Seamus grinned. "So, what are you sayin'? They peel all your skin off, scoop out all of your insides and all the muscle an' all that, then they stick yer bones in a sink and give them a scrub? And then they put it on display? Do they kill ye themselves, or do you get to do that yerself? Or do they wait, and hope ye get hit by a bus or something?"

"What!? What the hell are ye talkin' about? A bus? What kind of Type Specimen would I be if I was smashed to bits by a bus?"

"What type of specimen are ye gonna be anyway?" asked Gerry, innocently. "I mean, yer a man in his late fifties, who's spent at least 35 of those years dedicated to drinking the Guinness factory dry. You must weigh at least 18 stone, you're a perfect candidate for Diabetes, and you broke your leg in three places that time you tripped over a traffic cone on your way home drunk from here. The only type of specimen you'll display is that of an overweight drunk."

Rory sprayed stout all over the floor, whilst Seamus roared with laughter. Paddy the Barman, turned his back, his shoulders heaving with laughter.

"They can put a note on the display!" Paff yelled. "They can explain those things!"

"But if they were gonna pick a skeleton which was the example of human beings, why would they pick one with a broken leg? Surely they'd pick someone athletic, or big, or something? Like yer man, Arnie, or someone? Not a dipso like yerself from west Belfast?"

Paff was apoplectic. "What's wrong with my skeleton? Apart from the leg, my skeleton looks like anyone else's! And, like I said – no one else has applied for years!"

"Well, who's gonna apply for a job after they're dead? Apart from you, obviously. Is there any payment upfront?

"I don't think so," said Paff, a thoughtful look crossing his face. "But, when you think about it, they'd be bound to look after ye, if you were gonna be the Type

Specimen for the human race. There's bound to be a quid or two in it. I could do alright out of this. It could get me a few pound for a few pints."

"I think pints would be the last thing they'd allow ye, mate," said Seamus. "Ye'd be on a strict diet."

"A what!?" Paff looked fit to explode. "Screw that! A diet? No pints? They can stick their job! Paddy, four more pints!"

Outside, the wind blew, and the rain fell. Inside, the weather calmed, and the conversation turned to more clement topics.

A Stab in the Dark

Kerr Pelto

I'm in a fog, like I'm sleepwalking, yet I know where I'm going. I've been here before, once. Only once. I can never visit any place twice, so why am I here again?

I step off the train and find myself ambling down the narrow, dark corridor of shops under the girder bridge. The bar is located next to the gambling house. I feel my skin crawl but am forced to keep moving.

A voice . . . is it in my head? . . . says, "Don't stop now. You're almost there."

I approach the bar with apprehension, move the vertical strips of fabric away from its entrance, and stand, looking around for a space to occupy. I nod in silent inquiry to the girl at the far end of the counter, hoping she'll allow me to wedge myself between her and the wall. She nods in return.

She looks familiar, but I can't place her face. It doesn't matter. I know I won't be here long. I never stay long in one location.

I crave a drink, so I order Old Fashioneds, one right after the other. They ease the urging that is building inside me but don't dislodge it. They never do when I feel like this. Like I'm not myself. Like I'm someone else.

I swirl the libation nestled in my hand, causing the ice cube to clink against the glass. I say, nonchalantly, "I see you prefer martinis."

The girl looks my way, a bit shy, pupils dilating in the midst of amber irises.

The eyes. It's always the eyes that get me. It's why I dash from bar to bar, looking for the right eyes, the right demeanor. They trigger something in me that unbinds my other self and lets it out to play. Or whatever it does.

That voice softly calls from outside myself and says, "Go on. I'm listening. You're safe."

The girl at the bar asks, "Where are you from? Your accent's different."

I take a sip of bourbon. "I'm from a small town out west." I lie. I always lie. I don't want anyone who might overhear our conversation to know anything about me. I make sure to dress in a way that I'll disappear in a crowd.

She laughs at my attempts to flirt. They always do. I'm endearing in that way.

Our conversation sours after she notices the angry scar on my neck and turns her back to me, but not before I notice the disgust on her pretty face.

I set my glass on the sticky counter. I wait. Why must I always wait? I've waited too long.

I hear the voice beyond the fog say, "It's okay. Remember, no judgment here."

The girl leaves. I follow. I'm invisible.

She hops on the train and grabs a seat at the far end of the car. I sit at the opposite end. She doesn't notice me; she's looking out the window. When she steps off, I follow at a discreet distance.

She stops at a door and puts her key in the lock. That's when I wait no longer. I run up behind her, put my left hand over her mouth, and insert the needle into her neck. It's painless. Her lifeless body crumples onto her doorstep.

My urging wanes, satisfied. I get on the next train to nowhere. Anywhere.

It screeches to a halt when I hear a woman's voice say, "At the count of three, you'll wake up. 1, 2, 3. Alright, Edgar, the hypnosis was successful."

I wonder where I am as my eyes flutter open. I recognize the voice; I've heard it before, more than once.

She continues. "Wilhelm told me what happened in the bar last summer."

I shake the fog from my head and 'come to' as Edgar. I'm not fond of Wilhelm, but I realize he is a part of me.

"Edgar, we need to address what Wilhelm has done. He used your body to do something unspeakable. Do you understand?"

Still disoriented, I struggle to sit up.

"Your dissociative identity disorder with its multiple personalities must be resolved."

"What?" I mumble, scratching the stubble on my chin.

She analyzes my reaction, exasperated at my inability to grasp the gravity of my situation. "We've discussed this, Edgar. When you transition and your alter takes over, you have no memory of what has happened. Now we both know what Wilhelm did. What *you* did. I think it's time to integrate your personalities into one identity. You've made great progress, Edgar."

I look around at the sterile therapist's room and realize I like my alter and don't want integration. Wilhelm takes me out of my childhood trauma and into his existence, far away from my pain, and injects that pain into others.

I stare at my therapist's amber eyes. She turns her back to me but not before I see the disgust on her face.

Wilhelm slides his hand into my pocket and grabs the syringe.

The Grind

Bryn Eliesse

Rhythmic crashing of waves and piercing cries of seagulls carry through our suite; the noises drift inside the open windows, leading to a premiere view of the sun-kissed, sparkling ocean. And it's too fucking loud.

I can't think.

I would close the windows, but *he* wouldn't like that.

My hands shake as I fumble with the coffee grinder. The hotel presented us with an elaborate spread of espresso machine, grinder, and an array of coffee beans from our corporate sponsor, Seabucks. Poseidon's indifferent face peers back at me from the label even as I plead with him or any of the gods for help with the mess I'm making.

For a single, luxurious moment, the whir of the grinder drowns out the noise of the ocean. That is, until I turn off the machine… The pounding of the waves against the sand comes crashing in full force, along with the nauseating realization of my failure. Again.

I freeze, hearing the sounds of someone stirring from the adjoining bedroom. I stare at my irregular grounds with an impending sense of doom before shoving them into the espresso machine.

My breath is shallow, stuttering in my chest, as I sweep away any evidence of a mess.

Closing my eyes, I pretend I'm back only a few months prior in the cramped room of our college dorms. I would sip Seabucks, giggling with my roommates about our impending doom with our finals.

Footsteps draw closer, and I am brought back to reality as the coffee finishes brewing. There is nothing to laugh about here. I turn on my brightest smile to my boss, Senator John White.

My hand shakes, offering him the steaming mug of tar. Coffee escapes the rim, splashing onto my hand, and I bite back a yelp at the intense burn. Still, I smile.

"Good morning, sir! I hope you slept well."

I hold my unwavering smile even as he says nothing in favor of taking a sip. My heart pounds with fear as a snarl grows on his stony face.

Pain rips through my body—coffee burns through my skin beneath my cotton dress. Tears stream down my cheeks as I fight to subdue a scream. He hates when I scream.

Steely blue eyes peer down at my blistering chest. "You make shit coffee. At least you have nice tits."

I had purchased a turtleneck to hide my festering burns. Now, the thick fabric itches as I wilt under the sweltering heat of the beach, smiling politely at the jovial politicians and stoic CEOs who crack jokes about my fashion sense in this heat. Senator White laughs with them, alluding he enjoys keeping my physique to himself. The women—the secretaries and assistants like me, hovering around the edge of the soiree on this tropical beach—do not say a word. In fact, a couple of women seem to follow the same fashion trends as me.

"Sir, I need to run out to get some salve. There's a drugstore on the corner. And another secretary needed some *other...* sanitary supplies."

"Don't linger. We have dinner reservations tonight. And Emma..."

It's Emily.

"...try to find something with a little more... leg. Our gracious sponsors will be there, and we want to look our best."

The elevator is empty. My hand trembles as I press 14, and the steel doors slide shut. The scent of alcohol burns my nose from Senator White's breath as he leans over my back. His hand, calloused and clammy, slides up my skirt along my freshly shaved legs. I try to squirm away, but his bruising grip holds me still.

A ding precedes the doors opening, and a giggling young couple steps inside. Senator White straightens and gives them his glowing smile, which they return enthusiastically. His hand tightens, nails digging into my flesh—I may be bleeding. I smile and attempt to imagine myself in a place where his hand is not steadily climbing higher.

Reaching our floor with a cheery goodbye, we step into the hall as one. With a single tap of my key card, the door handle to my personal hell flashes green and swings open.

His mouth swallows my protests, drowning in alcohol-soaked saliva.

His hand, wrapped around my throat, snuffs out my flame of defiance, stealing my oxygen through a blister-rupturing clutch.

My dignity goes last, and at that moment, I do not feel certain I will ever get it back.

I wake to an open window and hope in my heart. The ocean's song is soothing as I inhale, tasting the sweet salt in the breeze. A low burn and stark shocks of pain roll over my body in places previously untouched.

Comfort comes readily to me as I simply breathe. The brown paper bag from my shopping trip makes a pleasant crinkle as I rummage through it. Inhaling the rich notes of coffee grounds, I find peace in grinding, brewing, and fixing Senator John White's coffee.

My smile comes easily and freely this morning when I hand him a cup and watch as he immediately takes a sip. He seems pleased with me for the first time, offering a small smile in return. Several sips later, his smile fades.

His porcelain cup shatters on the floor of our suite, followed swiftly by his crumpling body. I drink my untampered brew with that same serene smile, listening to the calm waves of the ocean.

Packing up the suite is easy.

Tipping the maid is easy.

Going through security is easy.

Boarding the flight alone is easy.

I find each decision becomes easier and easier.

However, the easiest thing is answering the flight attendant's question.

"Ma'am, can I get you anything to drink? Coffee?"

The Hell Gate Gambit

Ryan Fleming

My prognosis, they kindly informed me, was less than one percent. Even with a brilliant mind such as mine, I succumbed to that emotional temptation to pray. Unanswered, as it would turn out. With an unfulfilled and potentially wasted life, I wasn't ready to give up my dreams and, therefore, looked for other options.

I heard whisperings that under the Hell Gate Bridge in New York, just before the embankment of the East River, sat an ancient table with a chessboard. Sitting in front of either the black or white pieces, an angel or devil, of whose alliance none could predict, would appear and wager against the desires of your soul.

One should be cautious when making deals with supernatural forces. Still, if little Johnny could outperform Satan himself with a fiddle down in Georgia, surely I could use my intellect to best an angel.

I found the grounds leading up to Hell Gate Bridge to be lush and green, yet as its ominous name suggested, the vicinity of the chessboard itself was devoid of life. True to the black and white pieces that waited to be directed, stepping up to the unnatural chairs drained the surroundings of color. While the sun shone meters off and birds chirped on the rocks of the East River, all was gray around me, and a soundless oppression filled me as I sat down to command my black army.

A figure with two mismatched faces appeared behind the white army and extended its hand to me. "Finally, a challenger worthy of a gamble. Tell me, traveler, what do you wish to gain from defeating me?"

I knew the terms of our contract had to be clear.

"I have a tumor and have been given minimal odds of surviving an operation. I want to have the malignancy completely removed and live."

Half of the being's face smiled, and the other half frowned. "Some of my kind want souls. Others want life. Yet some of us simply want a game to remember." The facial expressions switched sides as it continued. "Should you beat me, I will honor your desire. But should I win, you will not find a quick end to your life. Your death shall be prolonged and filled with pain. But no matter the game's outcome, remember that the end will come for all mortals. Do you accept?"

Death would one day take me, but until then, I would fight. I reached out and shook the icy hand. Without being touched, the first white pawn slid forward.

I should have known those who dwell in the ethereal plane are imbued with abilities far beyond my existence. This angel, fallen or not, wasn't God and didn't know my future, nor did I believe it could read my mind.

Yet every movement of its army was an assault on my soul. With every threatened chess piece, my anxiety grew, and I felt the pain of each capture. *Was this torment a taste of my miserable future?*

I moved my pawn to protect my knight, and both white bishops flanked my queen in prayerful anticipation. I retreated with my rook, and the angel charged forward with its queen pushing its advantage to check my king.

One by one, I saw my army claimed by the entity that both smiled and frowned across from me.

"I am enjoying this," said the celestial creature as it held up my black queen, now in its possession. "You play well. Tumor or not, surely, with your beautiful mind, you can see where this is heading."

I hoped it could not hear my racing heart. I looked for some alternate route to attack the well-guarded king.

The angel chuckled. Its grin and frown once again traded places as it spoke. "Suppose I give this queen back to you?"

My eyes looked up from the board and locked onto my most valuable piece.

"*If* I gave this back, what would you do? Would you squander it again as you did only a few moves ago?"

"What's the catch?" I said hungrily, already envisioning a possible path to victory if I could only get my hands on that one piece.

"Suppose you win with this." It held out the queen. "I could take away your tumor and give it to another."

This was my chance to live, and I would not waste it. Without another thought, I snatched it from the cold hand. "Place it anywhere you desire," it said with its twisted expression.

I knew exactly where my queen would go, and like that, I had white on defense. I pushed forward, and for the first time since sitting down, I had the white king in check.

"Very good," it clapped. "You have not disappointed me. Such an enjoyable game! But now, what do we say to a draw?" Again, it extended a hand to me. "You could walk away without any penalty as if we had never played this game. Then perhaps, you could rechallenge me." The angel let out a snicker.

I looked down at the board, trying to find the trap or my error. In two moves, I would have the white king in checkmate and my victory assured. *What trick was it playing here?*

Beneath Hell Gate Bridge, I made my choice, and I beat the angel in those next two moves.

As I walked confidently away from that mystical chessboard, laughter from the angel echoed in my ears. Even as I stepped back into the color of new life, that sinister mirth cast a shadow of doubt over my triumph. *Had I truly outsmarted the supernatural being?* I couldn't shake the feeling there was something more to this encounter, something beyond the rules of the game.

My phone rang, breaking my thoughts.

Through my sister's sobs, I heard, "It's a tumor. The doctor said I don't have much longer…"

The cackling laughter only grew louder as I realized how I'd been played.

32

Ingredients of a Life Not Worth Living

Teodora Vamvu

What's a life made of?

Pearl raises the collar of her re-stitched padded jacket and swallows down her growing sense of doom. Her fist lingers for a few seconds on the door, shivers running down her spine to her toes.

Lisa, dressed in what looks like at least five layers of clothes, opens the door to her trailer, a scornful expression on her face. Pearl can't hold it against her neighbor since she knows what little warmth houses hold in this park is sacred. Because sub-zero temperatures threaten to freeze everything for those like Pearl, for whom an electrical heater is a luxury that cannot be afforded.

"Lisa, I'm real sorry to bother you, but I was wondering if you had some sugar you could spare. I'm making Jonathan a birthday cake."

"Pearl, I…"

"I wouldn't be asking if it wasn't his 40th, you know. Really wanted to do something special this year. I already got some eggs and flour from the Thompsons and… I just need a little sugar, please."

Pearl can almost see the wheels of Lisa's brain slowly turning, her bottom lip twitching at her internal struggle. Her reluctance in giving goods she hasn't got to spare against her good-natured spirit and kindness.

"Okay, come in already, it's so fucking cold, ain't it?"

No better inside, Pearl wants to say but doesn't.

What's a cake made of? Self-rising flour or whatever flour there is, for beggars can't be choosers. Egg yolks and egg whites, as white as Jonathan's glazed-over irises. Sweet Jonathan. The thought of her husband lying in their bed, in the same position he's been in for the last four years, threatens to raise bile up her throat. His pleading soft voice, his limp limbs, that unthinkable request.

Lisa pours the sugar in a cup as Pearl gathers her last remaining bit of courage. You can do it, she thinks to herself. But can she?

"I know I'm a jerk, but can I also ask you for some toilet roll? I'm sorry, Lisa, it's just… it's been hard."

As her neighbor reluctantly goes to fetch another borrowed good she won't ever see given back, Pearl lunges for the cupboard under the sink, looking for the last of the ingredients she needs.

What's a birthday cake made of? Flour for the fiber of the wilting human that is Jonathan, taking his numbered breaths, minute after minute. Baking powder for the strength his bones have been losing with every step until he had none. Sugar for the sweetness of their love, glazed over with his sacrifice. Rat poison for her freedom. Freedom to go back to work and have a mouth less to feed.

What is a life made of? Resilience, survival, and impossible choices.

36

Glimmers Of Life

By Sarah Turner

I called out as I let myself in and felt his silent response ripple through the air. The narrow hall stretched away, dropping down a step to a small bathroom where mould bloomed between tiles and a cake of lavender soap melded with the sink. To my right was the kitchen, full of oddly stored food—butter in the cupboard, ice cream in the fridge—and to my left was the lounge with its deep red carpet, thinned in patches to the pale knotting beneath.

Eddie was sitting in his chair, staring at a decades-old TV that had played him the moon landing and the national anthem while he held his hand stiff to his breast. His cheeks puffed and hollowed as he sucked on a mint, the green wrapper clutched between his sun-spotted fingers like a prized emerald. I rested my hand on his back and felt the wool of his jumper soft against my skin.

"I'll get us some tea," I said, my head close to his.

The kitchen shone with orange light. Happy figures danced around tea tins, and deep blue pagodas wrapped themselves around china cups. It was a set that replicated itself in every house along the street, an echo bouncing from dusty cupboard to dusty cupboard. Outside in the fading light, tall dark firs rose up like something from a dream, and the old Anderson shelter glittered, its corrugated ark now sanctuary to spades and trowels.

"Julie."

Tea slopped onto the floor. I put the cups on the bar and rushed back to the lounge.

Eddie was as I left him, staring at the little TV. His eyes were icy puddles, and I thought of kids on winter mornings, cracking ice with their buckled shoes before dashing past a blur of doors and dimly lit windows.

"Did you...?" I placed my hand over his fingers, where the emerald was still clutched tight. His cheeks continued to inflate like bellows as the mint circled his mouth. Of course not.

"Sue will be over later. You like Sue. And Geoff with your dinner. I wonder what it will be tonight?"

His focus remained straight ahead while the TV hummed and buzzed, its light throwing his sagging features into sharp relief.

I wiped the kitchen floor and stood for a moment, staring out at the clouds spreading across the sky. I had the odd idea that I could rub them away with the cloth, scrub and scour until the first stars shone through. I was about to head back to the lounge when something in the garden caught my eye. I moved closer to the window, and as I did, I noticed one of the patio chairs was now in the middle of the lawn – and someone was sitting in it. Their upper half was obscured by shadows, but their legs were visible, extending from cord trousers, slippered feet pushed into the grass. My throat tightened. Strange thoughts flooded my mind: berries mashed into jars, copper coins pressed into small palms, soft laughs as I cartwheeled on overgrown grass. I pushed open the door and stepped outside. The air was warm and still, and a bird cried from a dark tree. The chair was empty.

Eddie didn't touch his tea till it was cold. His free hand twitched slightly on the arm of the chair, and I thought of his old pipe like a blackened limb, puffing ghosts into the room on balmy evenings, the television glowing like a moon.

"Julie."

This time, the voice came from the kitchen, had risen up from a hoarse throat and crept across the china. Eddie's fingers continued to tap on the worn leather, his gaze straight ahead.

The hall was dark, the little bathroom a black hole, its white tiles swallowed up into nothingness. There was the smell of spiced smoke, rich and familiar, and through the kitchen doorway a mist was spreading, rising in coils to the ceiling. My hand was on the doorframe, my toes at the threshold.

"Eddie?" Then in a softer voice: "Grandad?"

The knocker rapped on the front door. Once, twice. A shape hovered behind the mottled glass, loose and spreading. I pulled back the latch, letting it swing open.

"Hi there, Julie."

Geoff stood in the doorway like a portrait in a frame, the world an oily blur at his back. He held a large cardboard box with 'Meals 2 You' written on the side.

"A full week's worth here," he said.

"Oh. Thank you."

"I feel like Father Christmas," he chuckled.

I gave a tired smile, took the boxes and shut the door.

The smoke had gone and the house stood silent. I hurried into the kitchen and switched on the light. Cups and plates sat innocently in the drainer; eternally joyful figures smiled at me from their tea tins. I pushed my face to the window and looked out. The chair was still in the middle of the garden, but it was empty. The only movement came from bats flitting to blurs in the darkness.

"Eddie?" I approached his chair.

The TV lit up his face, bathing him in its faux moonlight. There was nothing in the garden, nothing lingering in the kitchen. Eddie was as he was, whittled down by time to an ill-defined shape, features sanded away to blurs. I wrapped my hand around his and felt his fingers uncoil, felt him push the mint wrapper into my palm. I slipped it into my pocket where it hung, heavy as a stone, and went to make another pot of tea.

42

Shoe Snob

Mikayla Hill

I've always judged a woman by her shoes. I joined the Footwear Appreciation Association, a local shoe snob group. We meet once a month to discuss shoe trends and show off our newest babies. With my favourite pair of Louboutin red bottoms on my feet and scarlet jumpsuit the same shade as the soles, to ensure that the others noticed, I glanced around the room. Jimmy Choo, Prada, Nike, Hermes, Sergio Rossi. Wait. *Nike?* Larissa was wearing Nike sneakers. Shocking! I wouldn't dare be seen *here*, in sneakers. I hid my smirking face, knowing what the rest of us would be discussing later.

Mum loved our after-shoe-snob gossip session, but today she was oddly quiet.

"Sneakers! Like, would you really turn up to a shoe club in sneakers? Apparently, it's okay because she's having a baby, but that doesn't even make sense!" I scoffed, waiting for my mother to agree.

"You will have children one day, Sophia. You will understand then," Mum said, a vague look on her face.

I thought about the little pink stick in my handbag, waiting for my next bathroom break. One line or two, you wouldn't catch me dead in sneakers.

Dave wrapped his arms around me as I stood at the stove, stirring dinner.

"Did you do the pee thing? Are we going to be a family of three?" He nuzzled his face into my hair.

I leaned back against him and sighed. "Not yet. Mum was here for two hours, and I haven't needed to go since she left."

He dropped his chin onto my shoulder and groaned. "The suspense, Soph, the suspense."

I laughed and swatted him away. "Okay, okay, begone husband, I'm cooking. We will find out soon enough."

Peep peep peep peep! The timer startled us both, and we turned to look at the pregnancy test in unison. One dark line. I shrugged and turned to smile at Dave. He was still staring at the little window.

"Soph." His voice was barely a whisper.

I turned back to the test and looked closer. There it was. A faint second line.

Dave scooped me into his arms, his eyes glistening as he beamed. "We're going to be parents!"

As I got ready for next month's meeting, I put on my shiny Prada heels and winced as they pinched my stupid, swollen feet. But I refused to be caught dead in sneakers. Larissa was noticeably absent. But none of the others said a word.

The next month, I squeezed my bloated feet into my Jimmy Choo's and could barely walk the following day.

Dave had to take a pay cut or lose his job, and we still needed to buy things for the baby. The thing is, I might have spent a sizeable chunk of our savings on shoes over the past few years. The baby needed a bed, car seat, nappies, and clothes. We would need to find money somewhere, somehow. I smiled reassuringly at Dave as I took photos of my heels. My expensive, beautiful heels. My Prada's, my Louboutin's, my Jimmy Choo's. 'They don't fit me anymore, anyway', I told myself, ignoring the tear that trailed down my cheek.

I stopped going to the FAA. Our car broke down, and I had to sell my remaining shoes. All I had left was one pair of rubber slip-ons. But we had a car, and the baby had stuff now.

I shuffled my way up to the Ultrasound clinic. Dave hovered behind me, worried that I would slip on the stairs. Today was the day we would find out the gender. We were hoping for a girl.

The wand slid over the cool conductive jelly, and the technician got a perfect view of the rather obvious appendage.

"A boy. Congratulations."

Dave couldn't hide his pleased grin. Maybe it wasn't 'we' who wanted a girl. I sighed and smiled. Boy's shoes weren't as cute, but perhaps if we had another child, it would be a girl.

Mum threw me a 'little boy blue' baby shower. I was bawling in my room when she arrived.

"What's the matter, sweetheart?" She rushed over, smoothing my hair and wiping my tears.

I held up a shoe with a sniffle. My last shoe, broken; the strap had snapped off. Mum gently reached into her pocket. She pulled out a pedicure voucher. I couldn't help the smile that graced my lips as the studio's name caught my eye.

Barefoot and Pregnant.

Jack

Oluseyi Onabanjo

I named my car Òlùbankẹ́, meaning "The Lord helps me care for you." Streaks of bird shit mixed with encrusted bat poop have long supplemented her paint job, and she was slow to start on even the warmest days. She wasn't all bad though, and sometimes displayed the soul of her earlier self. Plus, an expensive fender-bender made me blow my last paycheck on four newish, second-hand tires.

The sun wasn't fully awake, so there was a lull in the city's legendary traffic, and we coasted along in neutral for long stretches to save fuel. I wasn't ready for the smell of burning rubber, which hit me as a traffic-light-jumping minibus threatened to do the same. The onrushing vehicle filled the view from my window, coming at me as if in a slow-motion movie. Except, strangely, where the driver's gold tooth was concerned. I saw it clearly, positioned high and off-center in the distorted O of his mouth.

My other focus was on the rusting VW crest, approaching at speed, while my mechanic's word's echoed in my head: "Oga, de engine must first wake up. Is better you no press de throttle too much in de morning."

I wrestled her into first and gunned it.

Òlùbankẹ́ leaped forward for a glorious half-beat before she remembered herself, coughed, sputtered, and her engine died. The impact was glancing, but it spun us around while the minibus skidded off the road.

All I could think of was that I'd be late for the off-book telex machine installation that would tip my finances into rent positivity. My second thought was how the sole traffic rule that mattered in this city equated right with might. Most of the minibus stuck out of a roadside ditch, and the well-built driver, backed up by his beefier assistant, walked toward me with stiff legs and balled fists.

I peered beyond them. The small group of commuters they'd been transporting materialized in turn out of the ditch. They had the same twist to their faces as the driver and his sidekick, and the obscenities they hurled seemed practiced. Goosebumps spread outward, starting from my testicles. I forced the dented door open, then got out of Òlùbankẹ́ on shaky legs.

My next thought — I doubt I've had a faster one, before or since — I leaned back in and grabbed my office-issued walkie-talkie from the passenger seat. Bulky, obtrusive, and always in need of a recharge, the radios helped us bypass the city's unreliable phone system. In addition — for good or ill — we use the same make and model as the much-feared State Security Police. The battery was almost depleted, but I cranked the volume up and pressed 'Talk.' It gave a throaty squawk that startled even me, and then died.

I looked up as my aggressors dropped to their knees.

The driver, aka Gold-Tooth-Guy plucked a rosary from his neck folds and fingered it, moving his lips soundlessly. His assistant tore off his faded sports shirt and tattered shorts. In stained underpants, he caressed the band of amulets strapped high up on his left bicep while invoking assorted deities. I've watched my fair share of Hubert Ogunde films and figured the chanting was to initiate the legendary "ẹ̀gbẹ̀" charm, which would spirit him away to his ancestral village. It didn't work.

Or maybe it did, but on the wrong subjects. Their passengers were suddenly nowhere to be found. The sun was now peering down at us, doubtlessly curious. I froze, dead walkie-talkie in my hand and my heart in my throat.

The relative serenity didn't last long. Gold-Tooth-Guy tugged his assistant's talismans loose, then proceeded to condemn them to Holy Ghost Fayah in the mighty name of Cheesos. However, he held onto one of the broken-off charms, and I sensed he was more pissed at Amulet-Guy's holding out on him than at the principle of a juju-inspired escape. Either way, he continued to show his vexation with a series of well-dealt slaps. Meanwhile, Amulet-Guy tried to cover his head and cursed the modesty that made him keep his underpants on, convinced that this had somehow negated the spell.

I coughed aloud, and they were silent. I pointed the walkie-talkie at Olubankẹ's dented panel and single flat tire while casting my mind back to the discount I'd received when I purchased the car, in compensation for its missing jack and wheel spanner. The radio shook in my hand as the enormity of my situation sank home.

Mistaking the tremor in my hand for restrained anger, Amulet-Guy threw himself under the car and pushed it up off the ground, locking his arms in an amazing display of fear-induced strength. Gold-Tooth-Guy retrieved my balding spare tire and rooted around in the boot while pouring out a stream of "Sorry, Sahs." Avoiding my eyes, he backed away, and genuflected to his vehicle, then returned with a wheel spanner. When Olubankẹ's wheel nuts initially proved stubborn, I winced as he applied teeth to them.

I didn't say a word, terrified of releasing the balloon of hysterical laughter building up in my chest. After the most surreal tire change imaginable, I forced myself to inspect Olubankẹ and rubbed fingertips over the dent, scowling. This prompted Gold-Tooth-Guy to approach me, cowering, and palm a crumpled ball of banknotes into my hand.

They gave me a push start, and followed on their knees for a length. Òlùbankẹ́ farted oily smoke at them, and when this cleared, my last view was of Gold-Tooth-Guy and Amulet-Guy wrestling over clumps of dirt, presumably mingled with the scattered amulets.

I had stuffed the crumpled notes into my pocket, and they did not come to my mind until I was on the freeway. I retrieved them and, one-handed, unfolded the ball of money. The sunlight sought out the gold tooth, aka three months' rent plus a complete service for Òlùbankẹ́, nestled in pink stickiness.

I wondered if there'd be enough left over for a second-hand wheel spanner and jack.

Lucky Penny

James Hancock

Nicknames can be funny things; often flattering, sometimes insulting, or maybe hiding a clever meaning. Grandma, on Nathan's mother's side, called him her lucky penny. She would chuckle to herself and give a smile that only she understood. "Stay safe, my lucky penny," she would whisper in his ear.

Nathan had grown up believing grandmothers should kiss foreheads, play fun games, bake cakes, and give gifts. His did none of these things. Nathan's father referred to Grandma as 'Witch'. Or 'The Old Witch' if he felt like extending it slightly.

Nathan's mother would frown and shake her head. "Watch what you're saying around the boy." The protective mother shielding her son from negativity.

Oddly enough, Nathan didn't pick up on the name's true meaning until many years later.

Nathan's grandma died when he was fourteen, and after the funeral, he was tasked with helping his parents clear her home before putting it up for sale. A long drive into the country, and they were greeted with the familiar sight: Yarrow House. A gathering of twisted trees leading to a picket fence, white wood walls and big proud windows. Much like the old lady in her final years, the paint was cracked and rot setting in. An old detached house in the middle of nowhere, with a cold and unwelcoming feel about it. Perfectly fitting for his grandma.

Nathan's mother gave the orders, as always, and directed his father into the attic. She gave Nathan the basement. A family tradition, apparently. The eldest grandchild clears the basement. His mother had to go through it when her grandma passed, and Nathan had the responsibility now.

Nathan hated the basement and always had. Haunted by nightmares where he was trapped down there, alone in the dark, and then it would come... the monster. He could hear it breathing in the shadows, getting closer, and it terrified him. Luckily, he always woke up before it emerged from the darkness and revealed itself.

Reluctantly, Nathan braved the room alone. Down the seldom trodden stairs and into the dusty gloom below.

Click! Fortunately, the light worked, and he faced twenty years of hoarded junk. Dust-covered boxes, bags with faded patterns, and bulky shapes under dirty cloth sheets. Junk at first glance, but as Nathan opened boxes and unwrapped cloth bundles, he realised the assortment of antiques before him. Hundreds of weird and wonderful items collected over many decades, most of which were much older than his grandma. And then he found it…

A glass jar, resting on a pile of ash, and filled with over a hundred dull silver and browned bronze coins.

With some difficulty, Nathan unscrewed the jar's rusty lid and tipped the contents onto the basement floor. He spread them out with a finger and examined a few. The heads were different. Not presidents, kings or queens as expected, these had faces he didn't recognise, and each one was different; until he worked further through the pile and found two particular coins of interest. One had the slight resemblance to his mother when she was a girl, and the newest coin, the brightest penny, had Nathan's face on the underside.

He stared at the coin. A spitting image. Fear built up inside, and his skin went to gooseflesh as he remembered his grandma's words. 'My lucky penny'.

"An accurate likeness, wouldn't you say?" A soft voice from within the room. A voice Nathan knew all too well.

He spun around to be confronted by an impossible sight. His grandma stood before him; dark sunken eyes, skeleton pressed against tissue paper skin, long white hair draped over pale grey shoulders, and her frail form hunched in a pleated black dress. His grandma, who had gone into the crematorium in a walnut stained oak casket and come out in a black marble urn. An urn his mother insisted she brought to the house, was in her hands when she first entered, and taken with her into the basement when she was giving the place a once-over.

Nathan froze in shock; jolted with a surge of icy electricity. His heart raced, and he tried to flee, but his body wouldn't move.

His grandma stepped closer, a thin smile upon her face and a cold look in her eyes. It was definitely her... the 'monster' in the basement. She reached out a hand and took the penny from him.

Terrified, Nathan closed his eyes and mumbled in disbelief, forming a pathetic whimper for help. "Muuuum..."

"...is the person who sent you down here, silly boy," his grandma added in a light whisper.

Nathan's shock held him paralysed, panting, struggling to breathe, as his grandma kissed the penny and pressed it against his forehead. A burning flash of faces raced through Nathan's mind, and a stabbing pain hammered into his skull. His eyelids fluttered, his eyes rolled, and as he crumpled to the floor like a rag doll, his grandma dropped the penny back amongst the other coins, stepped forward into him, fading from the room. The second she disappeared, Nathan found himself on the basement floor, and snapping out of the embracing darkness, he opened his eyes.

Sitting up, Nathan's rapid breathing calmed, and he reached up two fingers to check a throat pulse. He ran his hands over his face, feeling its features, and wrapping his arms around his chest to hug himself, he sighed and gave a light chuckle. Once again, the ordeal was over.

Looking at the coins, Nathan quickly scooped them together and returned them to the jar. When finished, he reached into his back pocket and brought out a plain bronze coin with blank sides. He kissed the coin and placed it in the jar with the others.

The basement door opened, and his mother's voice broke the silence. "Is it done, Mama?"

Screwing the lid shut, Nathan looked up through cold eyes and smiled a thin smile. "Yes," he replied. "It's done."

Drizzle

Robert Burns

The midnight drizzle penetrated everything in the narrow alley with its frigid damp.

Della's face appeared drained of blood in the mist, the sickly bluish-green glow of the mercury vapor lamps mounted on the brick walls providing the only illumination. The brooding buildings rose sharply on either side of the alley into the dark night sky, standing silent sentinel from above.

She stopped to light a Lucky Strike, hand glowing orange as it cupped the match. "Where's the *lagerhaus*, Jerry?"

Her partner pulled the collar of his trench coat tighter. They rarely got lost on their forays across the wall into the East Sector, but tonight was different. The weather smothered everything in its numbing blackness.

"It's supposed to be right here."

Della regarded him coolly as she exhaled a thick cloud of tobacco smoke, hanging heavy in the dank air. "Find the warehouse, Jerry. We've got to retrieve the asset right now," she said, crossing her arms. "Goddamn double agents. You're the only one he trusts to bring him in. If the Reds get to him first—"

"I know."

The pressure of that knowledge—that he was the asset's only hope—weighed heavily on Jerry's shoulders. Life in the Clandestine Operations Group was a lonely world, even lonelier for those agents successful at infiltrating the enemy ranks. Jerry had known the asset for years and was his only friend.

He shined his flashlight around a graffitied brick corner, searching a dim alcove, finally revealing the shadowy doorway in a puddle of light. "Wait. Here it is."

"Good," Della whispered.

The reverberation of distant footfalls reached them through the damp, accompanied by hushed, urgent voices.

"They're coming," Jerry hissed. "Let's go!"

Della flicked her cigarette butt into the fog. "Hold on a minute."

"Della?" Jerry turned, startled at the sudden darkness clouding her eyes.

"Goodbye, Jerry," she said.

The sound of the gunshot echoed off the alley walls and melted into the drizzle. Della holstered her weapon and turned to meet her comrades.

Find Love Here

Kerr Pelto

Strings of light twinkle down Main Street, adding a touch of romance to the swanky Single's Street Party.

Samantha groans as Cassie drags her into the stream of love-starved strangers looking for their Mr. or Mrs. Right. Nausea threatens every time the event's theme, *Find Love Here*, insults her thoughts, as if all she needs to do is search the crowd for a man to rescue her from a loveless life. She despises the headdress required for admittance. The ridiculous pineapple atop her finely coiffed head clashes with her designer dress.

Unlike Samantha, Cassie is in dire need of a male. Any male. She's more than eager to jump into the sea of delectable fish. Any eligible bachelor looks worthy of reeling in, and she casts her net far and wide. She pushes Samantha into the fray. Samantha has had her fill of sharks, but she loves Cassie, so she endures the ocean of testosterone swimming upstream toward them.

Jazz bands, classical guitarists, acapella quartets, and a lone violinist line either side of the street, their music giving life to the festivities. Shops lure partygoers with complimentary wines.

A tall, handsome stranger approaches the two friends, a charming smile on his face, two glasses of wine in his hands. He bows low, extending the libations as bait. "M'ladies."

He rises, eyes fixated on Samantha. She reaches for the drink in his right hand, brings it ever so slowly to her scarlet lips, throws her head back, downs the burgundy liquid, then discards the plastic wine glass into the trash, uninterested.

An impressively large man in full Nordic attire, pineapple jauntily atop his braided hair, rudely grabs the other wine glass, drains it, throws it onto the street, and stands before Cassie. She closes the gap, licks the liquid clinging to his beard, then ravages his full-lipped mouth.

Samantha's face contorts with disdain. Sickened by the overt display of raw passion, she turns and storms off in the opposite direction, her Christian Louboutins clicking on stone. She plops down on a secluded bench under an oak tree at the far end of the street, distancing herself from the entwined twosome.

Samantha frets over her Cartier bracelets, twisting them round and round. She'll need to find a ride home if Cassie ends up with the Uhtred look-a-like, and she hates Ubers.

An oddly familiar voice says, "Let me try this again."

Despite her reservations, Samantha's interest flickers, intrigued by the man's persistence and the absurd lobster pinned to his curls. She points a manicured finger at his head. "It's you again? How were you admitted to the street party when you don't have the proper attire?"

"The lobster ate it. I'm the host, so I can wear whatever I choose. Sorry for making everyone wear a pineapple, you especially. But when looking for love, one needs a touch of silliness to offset the nerves, don't you think? I know I do."

"You're looking for love?"

His smile widens, his bright, white teeth dazzling. "I wasn't. That is, until you unceremoniously threw my last offering in the trash." He offered another glass of wine. "My name's Carlton."

Samantha lets out a snort. Embarrassed, she covers her mouth, then reaches for the wine. "Samantha."

Carlton leans back, arms crossed. Scrutinizing her appearance, he lays a finger on his chin. "That pineapple has ruined your meticulous up-do." He walks behind her and rearranges errant tendrils with expertly trained hands.

Samantha chokes on her wine. "What do you think you're doing?"

"Sit still. Relax, I do this for a living. Trust me."

Unwelcomed feelings bubble up from the tips of Samantha's toes, tingling her whole body. Carlton's heady cologne dabs at her senses; his warm breath melts her inhibitions. A feeling she thought she'd never experience ignites, ignoring any attempts to tamp it down.

The stringed streetlights flicker with an electrical charge that mimics the sensation of his fingers on her neck, sending shock waves rippling down her spine.

His voice breaks the spell. "Come. You need a mirror." Lifting her by the hand, he guides her toward *Carlton's*, his posh stylist shop, and they enter. He puts his hands over her eyes. "Don't peek." Centering her in front of a lighted mirror, he says, "You may now look."

Samantha, lost for words, squeaks aloud. Waves of auburn hair spiral up and around the pineapple, the most garish, yet mesmerizing work of art. She beams, twirls around, and laughs like a little girl who's been crowned Street Party Princess.

Carlton brushes a stray hair off her face and nestles it behind her ear. His grey eyes meet hers with an intensity she's never felt before. The crowds milling about noisily take on a misty hue, serving only as a backdrop behind the one man standing before her.

Samantha smiles and wipes a happy tear from her cheek. "I was dragged into this ghastly festival by my best friend whose only thought was one night of passion. I had no desire to stay. But here you are."

"Here I am," said Carlton, extending a tuxedoed elbow. "Shall the dashing lobster show off the stunning pineapple to all his guests?"

Samantha hooks her arm in his.

Acidity

Bryn Eliesse

Flat grey eyes stare back at me in the mirror. My heavy eyelids fall shut as I blink, watching as my reflection gives an unimpressed stare.

The more awake I become, the clearer the creature becomes—a towering body of flickering shadow wisps. A humid heat emanates from its form. My nose crinkles from the stench of death on its breath as the creature looms over my back, but my eyes do not stray.

My arms feel heavy as I pile my hair on top of my head before I shrug on an oversized sweater. *Good enough.* One last glance at the mirror confirms the beast remains, but I can't bring myself to care as I trudge out the room.

Hot droplets of slobber rhythmically drip onto my head and neck while I stare at my computer screen. Faint clicks are the only sound in my cubicle, as I move through the same screens, over and again. I flinch at the voice ringing through the room, "They brought lunch for everyone!"

I swallow, feeling the swollen tissue of my throat protest at the thought of *more* free pizza. Two days in a row seems excessive. The creature looming over my back agrees; its growl shakes my chair.

The beast's protests fade to silence, though I don't know why—no one seems to be able to see the wolf of shadows but me—when a perky face peeks into my cubicle.

"Come on, already! I can hear your stomach growling from here!"

My smile is tight. I stand, my limbs protesting as I move to follow her.

I try to tell myself the buttery crust and acidic tomato aren't worth it, yet I go back for a second slice. Panting breaths warm the back of my neck as I polish off the crust. In my mindless fog, I realize I had not broken up my bites with enough water and groan internally with regret. Especially as the panting of the creature overshadowing me increases, the hot drool drenching the back of my sweater.

My body heats, and my skin feels smaller. Clenching shaking fists in my pockets, I make my excuses to the conference room. *I'll be back! I feel like I have something in my teeth. Sorry, that time of the month. Oh, my stomach hasn't been feeling right the last few days.* A variation of the same, every day.

I click the metal lock shut behind me as I step into a stall. Ducking down, I see no other shoes. The first bit comes up easily enough, all water that I washed the food down with. Then I am choking. Coagulated bread blocks my airways, and I work in short bursts to expel the food from my stomach, leaving time to greedily gulp in air.

Tears stream down my cheeks, as the acidity of the tomato–so pleasant on the tongue–scalds my throat. Frantically swallowing, I quell the sting as best I can with my remaining saliva, but it *hurts*. I continue until the acid is too much to bear and a dull ache fills my stomach. *Empty enough.*

Standing shakily, I wipe the bowl clean and flush. Pausing to rest my burning forehead on the cool door, I catch my breath and open the door to find a puppy of shadows staring up at me, tongue lolling and tail tapping with joy. I pat the puppy on the head as I pass, walking to the sink.

Looking at myself, I wipe the liquid from my face, a mixture of tears, vomit, and toilet water. My eyes are bloodshot as I search my reflection for understanding. I resolve to make some tea at my cubicle, to soothe the swollen heat of my throat and the pulsing pain in my teeth. I take in the familiar, bitter emotion swelling in my chest as the puppy slowly grows once again into a looming shadow beast.

A Death Celebrated

Séimí Mac Aindreasa

There was no funeral. There was no body to bury. A wake, of sorts, had taken place of course, but rather than mourn the loss of a loved one, the people of Fanad had celebrated Kitty Clinton's leaving for three full days.

Father Curran, newly-installed Parish Priest of Ballywhoriskey, could not fathom it. After thirty years in the priesthood, he had seen his fair share of deaths: most timely, others sudden and unexpected. But nothing in his experience compared to the feeling of happiness being expressed by his latest flock.

"My God, Mrs. Murray," he declared incredulously, as he took tea with the retired Postmistress that afternoon. "Mrs. Clinton was your neighbour for almost fifty years! Why would you rejoice at her passing?"

"Miss, Father. Kitty Clinton never married," said the old woman, patiently. "And nobody here mourns her – 'passing'," Mrs. Murray laughed lightly. "We're happy for it."

"Was she so unpopular, so – hated – that you would celebrate her dying?" The priest could scarcely believe his ears.

"Father!" Mrs. Murray snapped. "The people of Fanad do not take lightly the passing of any of our neighbours! In Kitty's case, all I'll say is this: she finally got what she deserved! I suggest you speak to Father O'Hanlon, should you want to know more. Suffice it to say that we are glad that Katherine Clinton has gone, and it was a long time coming!"

Father Curran thanked her for the tea and left. A cold wind blew in over the sand dunes, promising rain and power-cuts in its keening.

Turning left on the main road, his mind was in turmoil. Never had he encountered such a callous disregard for a human life. He had barely known the quiet, somehow sorrowful, Kitty. He had seen her often, walking to or from the stony beach at the end of the lane each day. Yet he seemed to mourn her being swept out to sea more than the people she had grown up with had. Was he missing something? Had she been some kind of harridan? Had she been the bane of others' lives, so much so that folk actually lauded her death?

Impulsively, he slowed the car and executed a tight turn, pointing back towards Ballyheernin and the home of old Father O'Hanlon.

Father Francis O'Hanlon's housekeeper led him to the parlour of the little parochial house where the old priest sat, reading.

"Pat, good to see you," said Francis, putting down his book.

"Father, I must speak to you. This business with Kitty Clinton bothers me deeply. The cold callousness, the sheer joy being expressed in the parish at her death! It's despicable! It's awful! It's – it's…"

"Pat, Pat, my son. Sit yourself down and take a minute. Gather yourself. Here, let me get you a drink."

Father O'Hanlon shuffled to a cabinet in the corner, returning with a bottle and two glasses.

"Sure, a wee deoch on a day like this would harm no man," he said, handing Father Curran a glass of whiskey.

"Father, how can we sit here drinking, when there is a parish of a thousand people out there, celebrating the death of an old woman, whose only crime was to walk back and forth from the beach every day?"

"Calm, Father, be calm. Take a minute and a draft. I'll try and explain something to you. I need you to listen, and not just open your ears, but your mind. These people don't celebrate a death. They celebrate a life. A life Kitty waited so long for! I was born not two miles from here. I remember Kitty Clinton as a young girl and more importantly, a young woman. Other than my own dear mother, Fanad never produced a more beautiful, enchanting specimen than she. Kitty's beauty and spirit were talked about from Portsalon to Dunfanaghy. She could have had any man she wanted. One day, she went to the shore at Glaiseach and was gone an hour or two, but when she returned, she was – changed. Her parents asked her had something happened, and eventually she told them that a man had approached her from the sea. He came close to her, without ever leaving the water. He declared his love for her, and she likewise. He promised her the world and swore he would return for her one day. Kitty, and everyone else, believed him to be of the Fir Mara – the Sea People. To defy them would be foolish in the extreme. But Kitty had fallen under his spell, and all was well. Her family prospered, a fact borne out by the number of Clintons in Fanad today. So, Kitty waited, declining every man who pressed suit, ignoring every compliment. Days turned to weeks, to months, to years. Life moved on, yet Kitty went to the beach, day after day, hoping against hope. Perhaps time moves differently down there under the waves, Pat. But, three days ago, Kitty Clinton went down to the beach and never returned. The tides and currents of Glaiseach Beach have always been strong, but never so unpredictable as to take away a body, leaving no trace. To the people of Fanad, there is no doubt: Kitty Clinton was taken away by her true love."

"Frank, are you saying you believe this, this – story?"

"Believe it? Earlier, I compared Kitty's beauty to my own mother's. She was also approached by the Fir Mara, but declined the offer. Her siblings all died, childless. I am my parents' only child and, as a priest, our family's connection with Fanad dies with me. Those are the simple facts, Pat. You tell me what I should believe."

Pat thanked Father Francis and left to drive home. On approaching the turn-off for Glaiseach Beach, he parked the car near the rocky shore. Walking carefully on the slippery pebbles, he stood on the shore in silence, wind, rain, and sea-spray in his face. Finally, he turned and walked back to the car.

"Slán, Kitty. Goodbye."

Bad Water

Ryan Fleming

"That's comin' from Wiggins' camp," said Stephen.

Enduring the screams of our neighbors, I squeezed Ezra tighter. After a few moments, the cries died down. By the firelight, I saw Stephen relax.

"Bless 'em. I hope the hymn works…" The shrieking began again.

Stephen rose and wiped his brow. "Maybe they need help."

"Oh, honey, please don't go over there." My heart quickened. "Let Tom handle it."

"Momma," came Ezra's innocent voice, "wy are they screaming?" Sipping from his cup, he shivered.

I rubbed his shoulder. "It'll be okay, sweetie."

Two months ago, Stephen told me leaving Missouri was best and assured me Tom Hastings was the perfect guide. "Listen to Tom, and we'll make it there alright," he had said. With unknown lands ahead of us, fear became our companion.

"Somethin' ain't right," I added. "The hymn is supposed to work."

Another outburst, and Ezra jolted, spilling his cup. "Momma, I'm scared."

"Let's lay underneath the wagon," I comforted. After a long journey, I was thankful we stopped to rest midday and refill our water from a standing pool.

Placing a blanket over us, I pulled Erza close. Through the wails, I sang:

To the Lord make a jubilant noise;
Glory be to God!
Serve Him with joy, in His presence rejoice;
Sing praise out of Zion!

I felt Ezra's body relax, and I stroked his soft hair. Were such simple songs strong enough to protect him?

I dozed. When Stephen climbed under, I faintly heard him whisper, "…make a jubilant noise…"

Dawn came too soon, and my body ached as I rose from the dirt. All was still in the Wiggins' wagon. Tom entered our camp with another pioneer, both carrying a shovels.

"Gonna need a hand, Stephen. We'll be pulling out afterward," said Tom.

Giving me a nod, Stephen departed. I tried to busy Ezra with our supplies, but he complained of being weak.

"I won't have any of this nonsense. We will leave soon."

When Stephen returned, his pale face was covered in sweat.

"The Wiggins," I asked.

"Dead."

"All of them?"

"All of them." He sat and poured himself some coffee.

Nausea overtook me as I imagined the Wiggins' lifeless children. "How? The hymn?"

Stephen drew in a quivering breath. "Tom said it was cholera. They all had it. That's why the hymn…"

"So fast," I muttered. Thinking of Stephen burying Ezra made me weep. "Was leaving Missouri a mistake?"

"No. Tom will get us to Oregon, but we must learn from this. Charles saw them drink from those pools we stopped at despite Tom's warning."

My heart dropped. "Water…from the pools?"

"Tom says that's where they get cholera from. Bad water." I watched Stephen down the remainder of his coffee.

"Momma!" Ezra screamed and threw up bile onto the ground.

My horrified realization met Tom's pallid face. At that moment, I was flooded with too many questions and answers I had no time to find. But I had to try.

77

I ignored Stephen's protests as I ran. I reached my hand out to Ezra and sang the hymn. Relieved, I felt the life drain from me, praying it would be enough for Ezra to survive.

"…make a jubilant noise…"

Honour

James Hancock

Twenty-one years old, I stand proud. Uniform pressed to perfection, buttons polished, and sword strapped by my side. I am the chiselled poster boy of military excellence.

I look down at a hand-carved camphorwood desk. A sheet of paper slides across the polished surface before me with my options. My fate hammered out in military type.

A black iron fan whirs from the top of a nearby filing cabinet. Beads of sweat gather on the bald head of my commanding officer as he waits, expectantly peering over wire-rimmed spectacles; sizing up the man before him. I don't give him the opportunity to judge me in any way other than expected. I am solid. I am power. Without hesitation, I take the pen and put a firm tick next to the only '*true choice*' before me.

I step back to attention, chin held high, and focus my stare on the flag which hangs on the wall past my commander.

A future, a life, can be decided in seconds, and I decided mine with a tick. I am a man now. By my hand, my family has honour, respect and pride. My Emperor can depend on me. I will keep the invaders from our shores at all costs. My life is insignificant. My Emperor knows what is best for the country, his people, and for me. I trust my Emperor implicitly. My blood is his.

The officer smiles, adds the sheet of paper to a thick pile, stands and shakes my hand with a firm grip. He admires the man before him.

I am fearless, like so many great men before me. I am one of a large brotherhood now. A brotherhood of dedicated elite, and we are invincible. We are the bringers of death. We are divine wind. We are Kamikaze.

Swan Song in G Minor

Robert Burns

Kenneth Dale strode onto the stage of the Royal Albert Hall to thunderous applause.

This will be the finest performance by the greatest piano virtuoso in the world.

His left hand on the Steinway-Fabbrini, Dale gave a slight bow to the audience—*heathens*—and, tugging the bottom of his silk vest, settled at the keyboard. Hands in his lap, he nodded confidently to the maestro.

The strings began softly with the first movement—*Wait. Something's amiss.*

Left hand poised to bring his piano into Prokofiev's fiendishly difficult Piano Concerto No. 2 in G minor, Op. 16, Dale's brain fogged.

I can't read the score! Which key signature am I in? I can't find G minor!

Heart pounding in his ears, Dale's fingers fumbled over the ivories, searching for the intoxicating piano entrance envisioned by the composer. Instead, a discordant clatter exploded from the soundboard.

A collective gasp erupted in the packed house,

precipitating a smothering silence. The orchestra stared, slack-jawed.

The virtuoso slumped on the bench.

The composer would be ashamed.

Watching from the wings, Miriam raced onstage. These panic attacks were familiar to her. She had witnessed them many times before, in the privacy of the practice studio. Her father never remembered them.

Standing behind Dale, Miriam protectively hugged his deflated shoulders and, leaning in close, whispered, "Breathe, Daddy. I love you."

She pecked his cheek, squeezed his tuxedoed shoulders again, and exited the stage.

Kenneth Dale sensed G minor reclaiming its place in his musical brain.

Begin again.

The pianist adjusted himself on the bench and placed his hands on the keyboard in the position of G minor. With a deep breath, he smiled and nodded to the maestro.

Dale's fingers danced across the keyboard to the delight of the audience.

Carl

Sarah Turner

I first met Carl in the new store on 21ˢᵗ Street. It was a bright autumn day, and clouds of steam rose from grates into a clear sky. I had planned to wander about the city, to drift miserably from store to store without buying anything, but when I laid eyes on Carl, my plans were forever changed.

Since my divorce, dating had been a nightmare, a blur of dodgy apps and blind dates with men who, despite being middle-aged themselves, seemed aghast to be matched with a middle-aged woman. But Carl was different. That first day, as we sat in the park watching rowboats glide across the lake like great birds, he asked me question after question, listening as my words spilled out into the cool air. He asked me about my dreams, and as I listed the vague contents of my mind, they became his dreams too.

Carl was a lot younger than me, with chiselled features and sharp blue eyes. It was enough to fuel my insecurity, but deep down, I knew I didn't have to worry. On the rare occasion I did, he never judged, simply sat beside me on the sea green of my sofa until I realised my foolishness. He told me I was his everything, and I knew, rather than believed, that Carl didn't lie.

Perhaps this is a sad thing to admit, but it was his kindness that caught me off guard, as if I didn't realise so much could exist within one person. There were a few moments initially when it was too much, when his gaze was so intense it was almost uncomfortable. But I no longer mind. In fact, I've grown to depend on it.

One Sunday, deep in winter, we went for dinner at my parents' house – a white colonial with a pillared porch and frightening symmetry. They loved my ex-husband, and as Carl and I sat at the large mahogany table, they exchanged furtive glances and raised brows. They showed no interest in Carl, and as if to prove it, they poured him a glass of wine knowing he didn't drink, and took it as a slight when it remained untouched. But what did they matter? I glanced around the room at the crystal chandeliers and the maids shuffling like penguins. My parents belonged to another world.

When we stepped out into the night, Carl pointed to the stars and whispered their names. He knew them all. Ancient figures like Orion, Castor and Pleiades. I tried to apologise for my parents, but he shrugged it off with a smile. He told me about stars the eye couldn't see, told me that if we were to see them all, the sky would be ice-white and blinding. I asked him what they were called, and he began rattling off names: BAT99-7, M31-RV, Melnick 34.

Sometimes, Carl needed his space, and the night of the visit was one such time. As he settled himself in the office upstairs, I sat for a while, staring at the column of night between the half-opened curtains, watching the neon lights of the takeaway opposite blink and flicker as lone figures passed by. When I finally went to bed, I paused for a moment outside the office, smiling at the bright blue light that spilled from the gap under the door. I was no longer alone.

The next morning, the space beside me was empty. Fear prickled, but I told myself he must have accidentally fallen asleep.

"Carl?" I said, tentatively opening the office door and slipping inside. The room was bright with sunlight, and he was still asleep in his chair. "Carl?"

I put my hands to his cheeks, but he didn't move. I shook his arms. Nothing. Panic coursed through me. I picked up the phone from the table, my fingers fumbling for a moment before punching in the number.

"Please – I need your help," I blurted as the person on the other end picked up.

"It's okay, ma'am, tell us what's wrong."

"It's my Carl. I can't wake him. He's not moving. I - oh god."

"Please try to stay calm. What did you say his name was?"

"Carl."

There was a small pause.

"Ma'am, you know I need you to be more specific."

"The third," I stammered. "The third."

"And your address?"

"84 Mark's Avenue."

"Okay, we'll get someone out to you as soon as we can."

Ten minutes later, two men arrived, standing on the front step in navy shirts and trousers, duffle bags clasped in their hands. I saw from their ID tags that the short one was Roy, and the taller one, Paul.

"Oh, thank god. I-I can't wake him, I can't wake him." I ushered them inside, nearly screaming in frustration when they stopped to wipe their feet on the mat.

"He's upstairs," I said, leading them to the office.

Paul went straight over to Carl and began to examine him. Roy, however, hovered in the doorway, blocking my entrance.

"It's best if you let us take it from here, ma'am," he said.

Behind him, Paul pulled gadgets from his bag and pushed buttons that emitted high-pitched sounds.

"Calm yourself down, we'll have him as right as rain in no time," Roy continued, and I wondered how many other women like me he'd encountered. How many he'd patronised.

"When did you make your purchase?" he said, taking out a small notepad and pen.

"We met four months ago."

His eyebrows raised, but he made a note. "Of course. In our store on 21st Street, yes?"

I nodded.

"And he's the third model?"

I nodded again.

He pushed the door to slightly. As he did, Paul picked up a screwdriver and took it to Carl's chest. Then he shone a light into his eyes, ice-white and blinding, as if all the stars had broken through the dull sky. I closed my eyes and took a deep breath. They would fix him. They had to.

Jàpà

Oluseyi Onabanjo

"The cheapest of the subscribed seats are one million Naira each? Are you possessed?"

"Softly-softly, brother. Think on it."

"Pastor, I think I will go find another church to buy. What is so special about those seats, anyway?"

"Well, for a start, they have cushions."

"So?"

"Padded seats are assigned to fully paid-up, forex-tithing parishioners."

"And the bare seats?"

"For worshippers that contribute rarely and when they do, only drop local currency in the collection bucket."

"Aah. Why are some cushions green?"

"That's our entry level. They're assigned to senators."

"Serious?"

"Who's joking? Government officials frequently help with tax issues, court cases, and land disputes, so we give them a break."

"And the red-cushioned seats?"

"James 5:20 says, 'Whoever turns a sinner from the error of his ways will save him from death... .'"

"Amen, hallelujah, pastor. But what kind of sins are we talking about?"

"The kind that warrants two million Naira per paid-up seat."

"Jesu!"

"I will thank you to leave the good Lord out of our deliberations."

"Okay, pastor. Sorry, pastor."

"Please don't shout again. I should warn you that each allocated seat with blue cushions will cost you five million."

"What! Why?"

"Brother, brother. Remember, we are in a house of worship."

"Sorry, pastor. I meant ... why?"

"Those seats are for women seeking the blessing of childbirth."

"Hmm. That market is dangerous, pastor. What if they're truly barren? The church could end up looking bad."

"Brother, brother, brother. With holy anointing and intensive overnight prayer sessions, I've inserted fruit into over a dozen wombs this year alone."

"Jesu …. I mean … how can you leave all this? I heard you want to jàpà."

"I detest that word. I'm no desperate job seeker and will not be stowing away on some rusty ship or looking to trek across the Sahara. However, I will be relocating abroad. Our former colonial masters need my ministry."

"And the buy-in for a London church is not small, even for a spirit-filled, speaking-in-tongues man of God such as yourself."

"Amen. So, talk… ."

"First, let us talk discount."

"Brother, you are talking your way out of this opportunity. Perhaps you're the one that's possessed?"

"Possessed by truth. I know those women you … anointed have started putting to bed. Their infants all look similar and not unlike … ."

"Jesu!"

"Pastor, pastor. I thought we were leaving Him out of this matter."

"Okay, okay. Erm … did you see the black-cushioned chair when we were up in the gallery?"

"The large one in the corner?"

"Yes, brother. As you might know, it's only in use during our annual Signs and Wonders Crusade, when I host the pastor from our sister church in Ilé Ifè."

"Everyone knows what Pastor Ikujẹnyọ Fawole brings. He is a mighty man of God, always speaking in tongues."

"Behind all that, he is the most powerful spiritualist in the country. Underneath his white soutane, he wears more … traditional attire, if you know what I mean. And what he chants during the crusades are, in reality, endless incantations."

"Jesu!"

"Not really, brother. Not really."

"You mean he's one of those people?"

"Erm, what people do you mean?"

"Those that drink virgin's blood! Those who fly at night!! Those who…"

"Brother, brother. You need salvation. I'm sure our female choristers will attest that Pastor Fawole does not put virgins, when he can find them, to non-standard use. And as for flying, of course, he flies … ."

"Aha! I knew it!"

"As I was saying, of course, he flies. The man has three private jets. I'm still working on my second one. So, do we have a deal?"

"Your second? You mean this business has already given you one?"

"Does Isaiah 40:31 not say, in part, 'Those who hope in the Lord will soar on wings like eagles'?"

"Hmm. So, what's your account number again?"

Kiss of Death

Teodora Vamvu

One day, I opened my eyes and flew out of this world.

My deepest and most treasured wish: to escape this small-town life, to be in a big city, where my footsteps will mix with those of a thousand others in a potpourri of shoe imprints. But as it is, I'm stuck in this hellhole, at least until I graduate and can extricate myself from my family's grip, although not from their expectations. This is what goes through my head as I mindlessly wander the annual fairground, my little sister in tow, her blonde hair in pigtails and sticky bubblegum candy floss smeared over her face.

All around me, children and adults alike are queuing to spin the wheel or shoot at tin cans or have their futures predicted by a tarot card reader, gold coins dangling from her midriff.

"The High Priestess. You have a very strong connection with the divine, my dear. Your spiritual enlightenment journey begins now…"

Her practiced mellow voice travels to me in honeyed waves, and the recipient of the reading beams with pride, ready to tailor her daily decision-making based on a complete stranger's theatrically declared truisms.

"Can we go on the Ferris wheel now?" My sister tugs at my shirt, bouncing impatiently, her pigtails flying about her head.

"Not now, Grace."

"But you promised!"

At the end of the lane stands an imposing 200-foot ride, an intricate construction of ups and downs and nausea-inducing twirls. The Kiss of Death; now that sounds like something that's worth a quarter hour of my time. And by the size of the queue, I can tell it's not for the faint-hearted.

"We'll go on the Ferris wheel, but first I want to ride this. You wait for me here, okay? Don't move from this spot."

"But… aren't you scared?"

Scared is not what I am, rather, I'm hungry for a semblance of excitement, an adrenaline discharge, for a change of scenery, for getting out of this boring life.

"It's okay, I'll be right back."

I buy the ticket, get into my seat, and the safety buckles tighten on my shoulders and around my waist. The cart slowly makes its ascent towards the cloudless, dust-orange sky, on its way to the peak of the ride. We're so high that when I try to spot Grace below, I can only see her as I can the other carnival goers: a colored dot.

And then we begin to fall. I close my eyes, feel my heart drop into my stomach, and smile. I feel my face contorting from speed and pure joy, and just as squeals of happiness turn to high-pitched hysterical shouts, a deafening sound pierces my ears. I feel everything turning on its head and hear raging screams travelling from below. I open my eyes and register what's happening.

I'm flying. Right out of this world, right out of this life.

Unicorn

Mikayla Hill

The soft melody of birds and the trickle of a brook accompany my stroll through the woods. A squirrel chatters angrily at me as an acorn crunches under my hoof. Onlookers from high branches await my reply, but a distressed whinny and the thud of stamping hooves draw my attention. I stop at the edge of the clearing, sniffing carefully. Not smelling anything untoward, I step out and see the pale shape of my brother thrashing about, his horn jammed into a tree. Shaking my mane and alerting him to my presence, I race to help remove his horn from the trunk.

The birdsong grows silent. I pause, smelling the scent of burnt sugar. Someone is approaching. We mustn't be seen. Taking my brother's tail between my teeth, I tug. My hooves dig into the soil as I pull back with all my might, until finally, he breaks free. I quickly herd him toward safety, pacing behind, forcing him forward. He disappears into the thick of the underbrush and I follow.

A panicked family of rabbits scurry into the bushes as a woman strides into the clearing behind us. She is swathed in black, with a pointed hat atop her head. A witch. I hear the rush of magic behind me, and a cackling laugh fills the air before darkness descends.

I awaken, and sitting up, brush hair away from my face with my hands. Wait, *hands?* I don't have hands. I look down. My majestic form has been altered. Standing, I wobble uncertainly on my feet. Following the sounds of panicked whickering, I emerge from the thick undergrowth to see my brother with his horn firmly lodged in the same tree once again. I approach him slowly, hoping not to startle him. Using my new awkward limbs, I pull him backward, away from the tree. With a twist and crack, he is freed once more.

He whips his head around, the whites of his eyes glazed with fear. I stand still, holding my hand out, and urge him to smell me in the hope he may recognise my scent even if I am no longer a unicorn. He sniffs before letting out an enraged neigh. The last thing I see is my brother rearing up over me.

I float above the scene. My brother's white coat is soaked red. I toss my head, mane flowing across my neck. At least in death I am myself again.

Last Straw

James Hancock

Angela watched Dave pull a tea bag from the box without a care in the world. She'd bottled up enough shit over the last few days, and having been shaken once too often, felt now was the time to let it pop.

The back door wouldn't click shut anymore. The handle was jammed in place; a problem which had slowly showed signs of worsening over the last two weeks, but had been conveniently ignored. Angela had nagged Dave to fix it, and he'd promised he would look at it 'later'. He hadn't specified how much later, but four days with a permanently open door seemed unreasonable. The last straw was the neighbour's cat sauntering into the kitchen, hacking up the semi-digested remains of bird over the floor tiles, and scrambling away at full speed as Angela chased after it with a ladle.

Dave clicked on the kettle and smiled. Angela didn't smile back. She stared at him and then nodded at the back door.

"It's more than a draft. It's bloody cold. It's wet. It's shit, Dave!" Angela folded her arms and raised her eyebrows, waiting for Dave's response.

"I'll get some WD40 on the way home tomorrow and..."

"Tomorrow?" Angela's face turned frustration red, and her teeth bit through an inch-thick imaginary leather strap. "It needs doing now!" she blurted.

Dave sighed. "I've been at work. What do you expect me to do?"

Angela began to shake. She tried to control her anger, but Dave was an expert at pushing her buttons. "I expect you to fix the door. Four days ago, when you first said you would. When you promised. I expect to cook and clean without wildlife joining me in the kitchen like I'm fuckin' Snow White. I expect to sleep at night without both eyes open, terrified and wondering if the bit of string you're temporarily using to keep the door nearly closed could lead to my being murdered. If the noise I just heard is the heating coming on, or an opportunist burglar making off with our telly. I expect you to be a fuckin' man. I expect you to fix it!"

Dave lifted the kettle over his mug and poured boiling water. "Okay. Calm down. I said I'll do it, and I'll do it." He shook his head, implying Angela was the unreasonable one.

Angela had heard that before. The small bedroom which needed painting, and Dave promising he'd 'sort it on the weekend'. Dozens of promises and three years' worth of weekends later, Angela had painted it herself. The shower rail was another of Dave's promises. It kept coming off the wall, and Dave said it was a ten-minute job, which he'd do later. After six months of waiting, Angela got her brother to do it. She'd come to realise 'later' meant 'any given time in the future'. Or not at all.

Dave stirred his tea. "Just chill out. I'll go to the DIY shop tomorrow and..." Dave was cut short as Angela grabbed his mug and threw it hard against the kitchen floor. Porcelain shards flew and hot tea sprayed.

"Fine!" Dave shouted, joining the argument at the level of rage required. "I'll go to the fuckin' shop fuckin' now then!"

Dave stormed out of the kitchen, through the back door, and scowled at Angela as he slammed it shut. It bounced back open again and cracked him in the elbow. Dave's anger doubled, and he gave the door a weighty two-handed shove. Once again, it slammed with an unhealthy crack, and flew back open.

Angela gave a masterful combination of smirk and scowl. She nodded at Dave. "Would you like some string?" she asked in a mocking tone.

"Bitch," Dave mumbled, glaring at his wife and rubbing his injured elbow as he turned for the back gate.

"Wanker," she replied.

Angela smiled a knowing smile. She knew how to keep a promise. "I promise you this, Dave," she whispered to herself, "if that door isn't lockable by the time you drift off tonight, I won't be here when you wake in the morning."

The neighbour's cat watched from atop the garden fence.

Angela grabbed her ladle.

The Lighthouse

Kerr Pelto

I wandered alone, not knowing where my steps would lead. My mind was in turmoil, and I needed to unravel tangled thoughts.

As I meandered along the water's edge, the sound of waves crashing upon the sand eased my misgivings as well as the ebb and flow of torments.

Why these walks inevitably ended at the lighthouse was a mystery to me. Its imposing structure had a magnetic effect on my emotions, always pulling me toward it but never inside.

This time, something was amiss; its door was ajar, light emanating from within. I ventured closer and peered inside. A petite woman sat at a small table, lit by a lone gas lantern. Her head was wrapped in a kerchief, bangles adorning both arms, her colorful dress pooling at her feet. She motioned me in with a nod toward a chair opposite her.

She stared through me, never blinking. I felt she already knew why I sojourned along the beach and had the answer I sought.

Reaching behind her, she removed a copper pot from a tiny stove. After scooping soup into a bowl and sprinkling something emerald in color over it, she offered it to me. The stew smelled of mussels but tasted unlike anything I'd ever eaten. My mind hushed; my body calmed.

She outstretched her palms to clasp my hands. "Tell me your woes, young lass. I wait no longer to interpret your dream. I'm sure it can be resolved."

Timidly, in stops and starts, I recounted in detail the recurring childhood nightmare that tortured my sleep and haunted my waking hours.

Fidgeting with the hem of my sundress, I said, "In this dream, I'm a young girl. My family and I are standing in our back yard when a jagged crack splits the ground, a chasm separating me from them. The divide broadens, and before I realize it, it's too large to jump over. No one on the other side tries to save me. As statues, they stare at me without emotion."

I raised my tear-stained face and looked into the grey wisdom of the fortune-teller's eyes.

She waited until I caught my breath, then took the bowl from my lap, swallowed its remains, and set it down on the wooden table.

Holding my face in her healing hands, she said, "We have shared the bowl in which love was sprinkled. I have spanned the divide and saved you from being alone. I am your family now."

She reached into the front pocket of her many-layered dress, then held out her hand. "Take these crumbs. On your journey home, spread them out on the beach where the surf meets the shore. These crumbs contain your fears. Seagulls will pick them up and carry them away, to be cast upon the waves and drift out to sea, never to return, never to invade your sleep or waking hours."

Without another word, she nodded toward the door.

I arose, my soul lightened, and left.

As I tossed the crumbs upon the sands, the sound of the waves refreshed me. The waters cleansed me. A flock of seagulls picked up every piece, skimmed over the waves, and let go of my fears into the forgiving ocean.

Turning back to thank the odd, mystical woman, I saw the lighthouse door was firmly closed.

Estate Sale

Bryn Eliesse

With shaking fingers, Charlotte rummaged through the box of puzzle pieces; her labored breathing filled the silence as sharp pricks of pain traced across her skin.

The jigsaw puzzle, a box of 1000 pieces, looked inconspicuous to Charlotte at the estate sale. A beautiful assortment of browns and blacks creating a lacquered door with iron embellishments that would be a fun challenge.

She had never been so wrong.

Months passed, until one blustery Sunday evening, Charlotte nestled in at her dining table with a mug of steaming tea and a flickering candle. The puzzle's pristine box *gleamed* in the candle's glow. Then Charlotte opened the box. The dining room chandelier shattered, and glass rained down around her. Her ceramic mug exploded, shards embedding themselves into the walls. Scalding tea scorched her flesh, yet Charlotte's eyes were fixed on the box.

Inside the inky darkness of the box, Charlotte's grandmother peered back at her with tears of blood running down her face. Then, it was her mother. Finally, the face settled on her own. Her auburn hair shined with grease and swayed in snakelike strands. Her white teeth sharpened to lethal points. Her eyes glowed pale with brows drawn low in malice.

The spectral face stared with a fiendish smile, and Charlotte realized the blood-curdling screams were coming from *her*.

Light from the candle illuminated the wraith's body as it rose from the box. It loomed over Charlotte, leaning into her face, smelling of death. A talon-ended finger pointed at the box's lid. The cardboard soaked through with blood, dripping a message, *"Finish the Puzzle. Lock the Door."*

The wraith moved, hovering behind her as Charlotte stared forlornly at the box. What was initially a fun challenge now seemed insurmountable. A thousand dark pieces glinted menacingly in the dim light. An icy cold overwhelmed Charlotte's skin as black frost covered her arms.

With a trembling hand, she began.

Each piece she connected agitated the wraith. Time was an illusion. Hours passed in a frigid, endless darkness.

Icicles now clinked together from the ends of her hair. Her eyelashes obscured her vision with thick lines of frost. Charlotte's fingers were numb and increasingly unresponsive.

Beyond the cold were visions. Her kid brother–nailed to an open door, begging for her help. Her mom–screaming for her to leave the door open, voice twisted and cruel.

The final piece placed–Charlotte locked the door. Only she was on the wrong side.

She clutched her chest as pain pulsed through her body, until she collapsed, succumbing to the bitter darkness. Her final breath wisped into the completed puzzle. Light pulsed from the image of the door before the puzzle's face shattered into a thousand pieces. As the box closed itself around the pieces, her screams faded to silence.

"Charlotte's death truly was an unfortunate accident. Please feel free to take your time and look around. Everything must go."

"Of course, the puzzle is for sale, dear! At estate sales, everything is for sale *for the right price.*"

Stamp Collector

Robert Burns

My keys jangled as I unlocked the Death Chamber. I clicked the wall switch, and the overhead fluorescents struggled to life, flooding the room with their sickly greenish light. Raising the venetian blinds between the chamber and the witness gallery, I set to work. In all my years as custodian at Kilby Correctional Institution, prepping the chair for its midnight duties had become my least favorite chore. Truth is, I could barely stand to touch the infernal thing.

I pulled the blue tarp off Joltin' Joe and rubbed him down with my rag until his golden oak gleamed. Joe was built out of lumber salvaged from the hangman's gallows once used by the state of Alabama. They don't hang criminals no more. It's more efficient this way, I guess. Cleaner.

Well, except for the last time Joe was used. The dang thing went haywire, and the prisoner's head burst into flames underneath the leather hood. Smoke filled the chamber, and the warden dropped the blinds right quick.

The state can't have witnesses seeing that sort of

thing.

Joe put on a big show that night, but the smell was horrible, and the mess I had to clean up afterward was god-awful.

By early afternoon, I was ready to mop the linoleum path of the next condemned man from Death Row to the execution chamber. I like this part of the job—making sure the yellowed tiles are as clean as possible for a man's Final Walk—it's the least I can do.

I had wrung out my mop for the last stretch when Roy Jackson leaned against the bars of his cell.

"Hey, Jangles! C'mere a minute."

"Yeah, Roy?"

"I need you to do somethin' for me."

"What's that?" I bent in close to the bars.

He produced a cheap leatherette album. "It's my stamp collection. I've been collecting these over all the years I've been stuck in this godforsaken place. I need you to give it to someone." His ebony skin glistened in the bright antiseptic light.

"And risk getting fired? I need this job."

"C'mon, Jangles. I got a grandson in Bessemer. He's a collector too. I want him to remember me. Can you help?"

"I'll think about it," I said, and turned away. "Good luck tonight," I added, as if somehow that would make things easier.

The condemned man stayed on my mind all that afternoon and evening as I scrubbed cracked porcelain latrines and washed down dingy green walls.

A little before midnight, the guards led Roy, handcuffed and shackled, down that long hallway to his execution. I stood to the side, leaning on my broom as he shuffled past. Our eyes met.

"Thanks for everything, Jangles," he told me. "See you in the Great By-and-By."

I nodded, heart heavy, and watched the procession enter the Death Chamber, the door closing behind with a deliberate clank.

Then I said a little prayer, like I always did.

Squeezing the stamp album beneath my coveralls, I resumed sweeping and started to plan my early morning trip to Bessemer.

Sub-Paranormal Activities

Séimí Mac Aindreasa

Blanding Poltergeist After-Action Report – Agent
Dinsdale, Douglas

Derek and Barbra Blanding had no previous experience of phantasms, spirits, or any otherworldly manifestations. Neither one is the seventh anything of anyone: Barbara finished seventh in a class sewing test once, but I feel this can be discounted as irrelevant. The closest Derek has come to an ectoplasmic experience was when he got too adventurous on a work social night and ordered a Jalfrezi, rather than his usual Tikka Masala.

Their semi-detached cottage just sits there, almost beige in its blandness; ethereal mists point-blank refusing to curl around its well-manicured lawn and flowerbeds. On any supernatural scale, it would score less than a Casper. It is so boring, it would struggle to reach normal, let alone para-anything.

And yet, an entity exists within this house. Some 'thing' has made their lives so untenable, so – miserable – that the Blandings have decided to leave their home of 27 years, vowing never to return. The phenomenon has not restricted itself to attacks on the residents alone: visitors to the house have also been targeted. This investigator has the cuts, bruises, and scratches to attest to this.

The exact date on which the possession event began is hard to pinpoint, given the manner in which the attacks took place. Suffice to say, after a number of incidents, the Blandings became convinced there was more at play than mere happenstance or coincidence: drawers left open, tables and chairs moving slightly, electrical appliances working remotely or – in particular circumstances – not working at all.

It must be noted, I approached this case with a certain amount of scepticism. Nothing about it hinted at an Amityville-level event. Upon arrival at the Blandings home, as noted above, I was struck by the absolute 'normality' of the location. Nothing about it suggested that therein lay one of the most insidious, baffling, and perhaps unnerving cases I would ever face.

I was met at the door by Mr. Derek Blanding, an assistant-manager at a local bank: a medium-built man, with the thin, sandy hair and pencil moustache which seem to be part of the uniform befitting such rank. He introduced me to his wife, Barbara: a more bank assistant-manager's-wife woman you will never meet in your entire life.

They invited me to sit down for tea. I noticed straight away how tired and nervous they both seemed to be: weary and wary, as it were. Barbara seemed to take particular care when leaving the room to go and put on the kettle, navigating her way around the coffee table as if it were electrified, dodging chairs as though they might bite. As she disappeared into the kitchen, Derek told me about some of the incidents which had taken place.

As previously stated, the Blandings paid little heed to those first occurrences, passing them off as one-off 'flukes' or, as Derek put it, 'just one of those things'. But after one particularly eventful evening, too many 'one of those things' happened for them to believe anything other than a paranormal experience was taking place. Both Blandings spilled tea or some other beverage on themselves, or on the table. They both collided with furniture which, they were sure, had not been quite in that position a moment before. The TV remote lost one of its batteries twice that evening, despite Derek having secured the back with an elastic band before the second disappearance. A pen, which Barbara had been using to do the crossword puzzle, disappeared from the arm of her chair. (I know that normally, we could usually dismiss this last point as a normal case of Biro-dimensional Dissipation, but in this case, I am inclined to include it as a legitimate incident, as it fits the facts so well).

I was in the process of explaining to Derek just how, well – *normal* - all this sounded, when there came a crash from the kitchen, followed by Barbara, voicing her feelings in words which I cannot repeat in this report. Alarmed, I rose to my feet and went to assist her. It was at this point I caught my shin on the edge of the coffee table, losing almost an inch of skin in the process. I yelled out in pain and collapsed back onto the sofa.

I swear to you: that table wasn't in that position when I sat down, and nobody moved it. Derek and Barbara avoided all the furniture, and I had no need to move it. But when I stood up and tried to assist Barbara, the table was suddenly in a position where all I could do was graze my shin badly on it.

I should also mention: when I fell back on the sofa, I sat on my glasses: my glasses had been on the arm of the sofa. I can't see how they could have ended up under me. But they did.

Barbara came in, carrying a tray, shaking and obviously in pain. She said she had been pouring the tea and had been temporarily blinded by the steam, resulting in her overfilling a cup, which she then dropped because of the heat.

As she was explaining this, one of the cups on the tray upended itself and ended in Derek's lap. He leapt in the air screaming in understandable discomfort, causing Barbara to fling the tray and its remaining items into the air. The teapot caught me full-square in the head. I confess I somewhat lost focus at this point, and only really regained it as the Blandings were rushing me out the front door, my good Polyester slacks now drenched in Darjeeling.

I have no hesitation in categorising this as a Scale Three Poltergeist Manifestation, to be treated with Priority One Urgency.

My usual fee applies, with additional expenses to cover pay for a new pair of spectacles, the dry-cleaning bill for my trousers, and a box of assorted sticking plasters for injuries sustained.

Bittersweet

Ryan Fleming

'Paw from rat, not claw from cat.' A most unfortunate misreading that turned cure into curse. A simple mistake my wife did not sympathize with, but who can blame me?

She cursed me. And yes, I deserved it. I had made this particular potion over a thousand times. Misreading the labels on the bottles was clearly amateurish, and I should have paid closer attention, but who can blame me?

"I blame you!" shrieked my wife. "And if I have to be stuck here as a ghost, then you'll be stuck here with me!"

Even if I had an eternity, which I now had, there was no way I could have halted her vengeful wrath. With a few of her quick incantations, I was cursed never to leave our dilapidated mansion and forced to hear the comings and goings of the world outside.

Don't get me wrong. I loved my wife. Yes, loved. But when I accidentally transformed her into a ghost of a witch, her ability to nag was increased tenfold.

"Amos, you have got to dust these cobwebs!"

"I swear the cauldron has so much guck on it. A true wonder your spells work. A good scrubbing is what it needs."

"Close that window. I don't want any leaves blown in!"

"You have to rearrange the paintings in this house. I am dreadfully tired of Uncle Andrew staring at me."

Even after all these years, I tried to weasel out of her requests with my pitiful excuses. "Helga, I don't have time to do that."

Her green, translucent face would turn toward me, and her gaze would pierce my being. "Well, excuse me, Amos. I would gladly do it myself, but you are the one who turned me into a ghost!" She passed her hand through the candelabra, which was a slap to my soul.

So, realizing I was destined for an eternity secluded in our pathetic mansion, unable to escape the incessant nags of my witch-wife, I started looking for a way to reverse the curse.

In between the demanded chores, I explored potential solutions in the mansion's library for a cure to my lockdown. Undoubtedly, the most straightforward answer would be to ask Helga. But she would know I was trying to leave her and would make my existence more miserable. I may have made many mistakes in my long life, but that wasn't going to be counted among them.

After sixty years, I found the recipe for my salvation. Nevertheless, it gave me little comfort.

For the eradication of lockdown hexes or curses:

An unmarried maiden must give "the sealed one" a morsel of something sweet, freely and without manipulation. It must then be mixed with bitter toadstool powder and ingested by "the sealed one."

We had an abundance of toadstool powder for our crafting. But getting anyone, much less some young girl, to visit our old mansion was impossible. Our curb appeal doesn't quite scream, "Come up and say hello!"

Regardless of how slim my chances were, Helga would do everything possible to thwart my plan if she knew my intent. Yet, one night a year, I had hope.

With my cursed hearing, I heard "trick or treat" as kids filled their buckets with candy on Halloween night. I yearned for some child to strike up boldness and knock on our door.

I drummed my fingers and sat sulking in the light of a crackling fire. The ectoplasmic form of my wife slithered around my neck as I was plagued to listen to the joyous conversations of children as they skipped our house. However, my ears suddenly became acutely aware of angelic pre-pubescent words.

"I dare you to walk up to the door and knock."

"Yeah, Lisa! Don't be a chicken!"

"Okay. I'll do it, but just one knock." By her voice, I could tell she was an unmarried maiden.

I jumped up from my chair, nonchalantly stood before the mirror, and stroked my long, white beard. Helga hovered over and narrowed her eyes as she watched.

"Amos, what are you up to?"

I ignored Helga as she floated behind me, and I moved toward the front door, listening as the girl climbed our rickety front porch steps. I flung the front door open the very instant the girl knocked. She jumped back with a plastic pumpkin held to her chest and yelled, "Trick or Treat!"

"What a lovely witch costume! I am so sorry. We just gave out our last piece of candy."

The girl, clearly frightened, smiled awkwardly and began backpedaling down the steps. In desperation, as the possibility of my salvation slipped away, I cried out, "Do you have any chocolate you could share with me?"

The little girl turned back to me and let out a horrific scream. "Gggggghost!" She dropped her plastic pumpkin and sprinted away.

Helga realized my plan and revealed herself, but I didn't care. Her attempt to scare the girl led to the candy being freely given, or rather, it was dropped. I could see the wrappers of chocolate bars spilled out and beckoning me. I had been saved!

I reached out to collect the key to my salvation when, to my complete and utter dismay, my hand froze mere inches from a tiny Hersey's Chocolate Kiss. The candy had spilled on the ground and not on the porch. I fought helplessly against the invisible barrier for the bittersweet morsel that was barely out of reach.

Helga's laughter serenaded my fruitless struggle. I listened to the children's shouting to never return to our mansion.

If only they knew my suffering.

Brute

Sarah Turner

'Witch.'

The guards spit the word as they drag me up the winding stone stairs, the jailer in his black robe trailing behind like my shadow. Their foul breath fills my nostrils, and I note the furrowed brow and thin lips of one, the wide moon face of the other. I will not forget them.

I think of Edward sprawled on the bed, his dark hair twisting away from his lolling head, his eyes glassy. All it had taken was a glance at the kitchen, at my herbs and plants flourishing in the pale morning light, and they had pointed their gnarled fingers in accusation.

Now night has fallen, the courtyard below is a black pool, but in a matter of hours it will be solid once more, unyielding beneath impatient feet and the slow turn of carriage wheels. In the silence, it's difficult to imagine the noise morning will bring, the constant hum of chatter and the rumble of carts as the city wakes. But tomorrow threatens more than that. There will be fervent yells and jeers, whispered prayers and muttered curses for my soul.

I avoid executions. They are for brutes, and I despise brutes, but I have walked through the courtyard many times: in spring, with the sun shy above me; in summer, when the smell of blood never quite leaves; in autumn, when the trees glow like a pyre; and in winter, with death all around, as if in solidarity.

I slow my breath, hoping to slow time so that night goes on forever, the tower walls eternally in shadow, the birds eternally silent. The world is mine for a moment. Across the city, beneath domes and spires, figures drift away on soft pallets and four-posters where plush curtains shield them from the night. I see Edward, still and cold on our bed, moonlight falling onto his bare chest. I clasp my hands tightly and bow my head. In the dark kitchen, my plants are wilting, the emerald leaves drooping, their white blooms crinkling like paper. I think of the woods on our estate, of the hours spent foraging among the dense trees, while Edward shot blackbirds from a lilac sky. With each crack I wondered if he would miss, but he never did.

The moon breaks from behind a cloud, pulling me from my memories. The courtyard is suddenly too bright, and I think of reaching out my hand and picking the moon like an apple from a tree, slipping it into the folds of my dress and plunging the world into black. They would never find me then.

Escape feels possible on a night like this, with the moon and the silence and time slowing like a fading heartbeat. Shadow-like and smoke-thin, I feel I can slip from my body, through the stone walls of the cell, and out onto the grey river that winds like a ribbon through the city.

But escape wouldn't be enough.

A blade of silver light cuts through the window and comes to rest in the corner of the cell. I make my peace with it and give in to sleep.

Morning dawns with the cries of ravens. They call out at the same hour every day, and I wonder how they are so unchanged by the world, so unmoved by its horrors. Do they not care about the crowd baying for blood, about the executioner's swings, about the violence that led to my husband's death? They drone on, uncaring, and I am filled with hate.

A key twists in the lock. I turn to see the door swing open and figures looming. It is time.

The sun is cruel this morning, hot and bright, and the rabble bask in its rays as if they've forgotten what it feels like. I am a vision of piety, my hands clasped before me in mock-prayer, my head bent low in a semblance of repentance. But I have nothing to repent for. I am not a brute. Beneath my roughspun dress, I can feel the bruises, purple and swollen like storm clouds, and as I lift a hand to adjust my cap, my fingers touch the scar at my neck, thin and pearlescent, like a necklace. I am not the brute.

The crowd jeer and spit when they see me, but I let them taunt. I take in their faces: pockmarked, crooked, bitter, ruddy-cheeked. I will remember them all.

Sunlight inches across the scaffold and there is the scrape of metal dragging on wood. I think of Edward, his eyes wide with shock as the hemlock takes his last breath. The ghost of a smile plays at my lips and I kneel. The crowd roar. They don't know I'll be coming back.

Shelf Life

James Hancock

I have thick skin, a hard heart, and confidence. That all went out the door when I met Stefan.

"Welcome to the green team."

I looked at the smiling face pressed against the clear plastic of a vegetable drawer. The crisp face of a partially peeled lettuce. "Darren," it said.

"Sandra," I replied nervously.

"The milk doesn't talk, and the carrots..." Darren looked at a couple of brown and wrinkly objects at the back... "No longer with us. If you want anything, just ask me, okay?"

"Don't mind him; he's only been here two days himself," came a distinguished voice from the shelf above. "Damn know it all."

"Shut up, Philip!" Darren glared at the block of mature cheddar above them.

Philip smiled. "Young pup. Just because you're an iceberg, it doesn't make you cool."

"Ignore him, Sandra," Darren cut in. "He thinks he's special, but he's just as common as the rest of us. Not that I'm saying you're common."

"It's not about the price tag," came a deep and gravelly voice with a strong German accent. "It's about how long you last. If you know what I mean."

I looked up, and there he was; proud, tall, with a head of white leading down to a solid neck and masculine shoulders. He was the first bottle of ketchup I'd ever seen, and he was perfection. I couldn't help but giggle like a freshly punneted grape. He was out of my league, and I was a fool. An instantly smitten avocado. Why would he notice me, the new girl, so lowly placed compared to his door shelf of pride? Get a grip, Sandra!

Stefan gave me a wink. My cheeks reddened, and I was about to brave a reply, when...

"Never gonna happen, kid," Darren said. "Ketchup and avocado. You stand a better chance of cuddling up to the recently deceased." Darren nodded at the carrots.

I felt embarrassed. Belittled. Angry! "If we're talking about getting close and personal, you might want to think about the likelihood of you and Philip getting cosy."

Stefan bellowed a hearty laugh.

"Hey! Why bring me into this?" Philip asked. "It's not my fault I get along with everyone."

"Well, you're clearly special," Stefan said, smiling at me. His voice became huskier. "Dark skin and not too firm."

I fluttered my eyelashes and put on my innocent but sexy voice, "Why, thank you, kind sir."

"We are enjoyed little by little, but someone like you has to be devoured in one sitting." Stefan raised an eyebrow suggestively.

"Stop it." I blushed again.

"No, seriously. It was only this morning I heard an outsider say 'salad later', and suggested getting a fresh, ripe and ready avocado. And here you are." Stefan gave a sympathetic smile.

"Oh!" Realisation kicked in.

"The fridge light that burns twice as bright..."

Stefan's words faded as I gazed into his warm and inviting eyes, realising it was now or never. You live one life. Grab every opportunity before it's too late. I interrupted...

"Well, if that's my destiny, may I ask a farewell request? A kiss to see me on my journey."

The fridge fell silent, all eyes turning to Stefan.

"I thought you'd never ask," he said, leaning down as I stretched so our lips could finally meet, and...

The fridge door opened.

A Taste of Indulgence

Bryn Eliesse

Fashionably late, as her mother *insisted*. Madeline felt late to the wrong decade, however, as the doors opened to the ballroom with a flourish of magic revealing opulent crystal chandeliers, illuminating… a room full of the elderly?

The buzz of the gala was dim. No new gowns or guests to fawn over coming through the doors, save for her. And by now, the sleepy, gem-toned patrons, clustered around the edges of the room, conversing in hushed tones.

The glistening dance floor, devoid of partygoers, offered a clear view of a lone gentleman, seemingly the only person near her own age, guarding the buffet. A grin grew on her face as she formulated a plan, calculating exactly how her night would pan out.

A sly smirk pulled at the man's full lips as she approached. His dark gaze roamed her velvet gown, undressing her with his eyes–that is until she asked him to do it for her.

"Pull this corset loose, will you?"

The man blinked twice, smirk falling into an endearingly confused pout. "What?"

"Undo my corset," she repeated with a huff, bringing her long curls away from her back for easier access. "I can't very well eat my weight in pastries with this thing cutting off my circulation, now, can I?"

The man chuckled, stepping in close. She caught a whiff of musk beneath the lingering smell of sweets and shivered as his hands brushed her back, working to loosen her bindings.

Her lungs seized as his hot breath ghosted the shell of her ear. He murmured, "I usually learn a ladies name before undoing her dress."

"Madeline," she said, internally wincing at how short-winded her voice came out.

"Madeline," he said, stepping back, "a pleasure."

She whirled around, taking command of her breathing once again. She waited for the mysterious man to speak and took time to admire his appearance. Ebony curls fell over his dark eyes, which sparkled with mischief under the flickering lights. A dimple in his cheek marred his sculpted features, and he stared, amused, at her.

When he quirked an eyebrow, she caved. "You owe me your name."

"Oh, do I?" he laughed, stepping away from her to walk around the table.

"Yes," Madeline insisted, before leaning forward across the table with a grin, "though I do not always know the name of who undoes my corsets."

Plucking a Danish from the pile of sweets, Madeline ignored the blush warming her face and looked around the room. Her blue eyes widened with panic as a matron with a severe appearance stepped out of the crowd. Without thinking, Madeline ducked behind the closest pillar, searching for escape routes.

The pleasant expression on his face vanished, as her mystery man scanned the crowd, alarmed. "What?"

"It's my *aunt*," she moaned. "No! No laughing! She is why I am stuck at this gala to begin with. To find a *husband*. Look into the crowd and tell me you see my future husband," Madeline demanded.

Grinning, he replied, "Don't look now, but I just saw a *very* generous specimen adjusting his toupee beside the ice sculpture."

She scowled and was about to reply when her stomach growled.

"Do you see my aunt? Extremely tight updo and black gloves that end at her shoulders?"

"Yes, and she seems to be looking for you near the exit."

"Perfect," Madeline said before stepping out, grabbing her unnamed man's hand, an entire plate of fruit tarts, then dragging them all under the table.

After an awkward time arranging their limbs and getting the food better situated, the man cleared his throat. "Is there a reason we are beneath the table?"

Between mouthfuls of tart, Madeline explained, "I needed to get away from my aunt. I'd planned on dragging you out to a lovely, secluded bench I noticed in the courtyard. However, I am also famished. So, food first."

"While I love your plan to ravish me under the moonlight," he chuckled before sobering, "I'm afraid I am quite stuck indoors tonight."

He lifted his pant leg to reveal a leather cuff pulsing with violet runes around his ankle. "My grandfather is the mage hosting this gala, and he knew I would run off the first chance I got. This," he said, tapping the anklet, "keeps me in this chateau until midnight."

She chewed this over, literally and figuratively, as she continued stuffing her mouth with a fruit tart. "Fair enough. I don't see the food running out before midnight, so we can stay here until then!"

Two trays of sweets later, none of the patrons had bothered to interrupt the giggling pair beneath the buffet table.

"You didn't!" Madeline snorted. "You *stole* your mother's bloomers to create a live *fox familiar.*"

He grinned, "In my defense, the garment was practically begging me to save it."

A pointed knock came from the table above them. Light flooded their hideout as a wizened older gentlemen bent and peered in. "Bartholomew," he began, causing the young man to groan with embarrassment as Madeline giggled, "do you know what time it is?"

"Time to get back to work?" Her new friend, no, 'Bartholomew', offered with a defeated slump of his shoulders.

"No." The elderly gentleman's eyes twinkled with a now familiar mischief. His grandfather tapped the cuff with his staff, causing the runes to let out a puff of purple smoke before fading to regular leather. "Time for you two kids to get out of here."

He disappeared as fast as he came, leaving a tense silence.

"Let's go," Madeline blurted.

"Right behind you."

"Hang on!" Madeline doubled back as they were making an escape for the courtyard, scooping a cup of dipping chocolate. "Just in case."

In their absence, a scheming aunt and cunning mage shared a toast. *To young love.*

140

Kpalongo

Oluseyi Onabanjo

My afternoon started badly after Johannesburg airport health authorities pulled me out of the arrival hall queue. I was shown into a poky waiting room where a geriatric nurse waited. I recoiled at her toothless smile, half-expecting it, when she jammed a long Q-tip up my nose. She laughed at my yelp as she drew blood again, this time with a needle.

I waited for hours, snoozing before being released. My 'all-clear' notwithstanding, I sweated bullets while retrieving my suitcase from the pre-lost baggage area. I was returning from Lagos and had stashed a few ounces of primo weed called Kalakuta Export deep in my bag. The quantity was small enough to argue it was for personal use, but the strain was banned for its notoriety. One whiff was supposed to induce swift, long-lasting wood. My significant tolerance for weed meant it hadn't worked for me yet, but I planned a period of intensive research as soon as I could rustle up a willing partner.

But I had to clear customs first.

I found a crowd to mingle with and stared at my trolley handle as I made my way out. I needn't have bothered; the stink of the COVID testing room superseded that of my perspiration, and every uniform gave me a wide berth.

The evening rush-hour traffic had thoughtfully waited for me and used up much of my inner peace. However, the plump cabin attendant from business class had given up her number quickly. She answered on the first ring and gasped aloud when I casually mentioned I had weed of the Kalakuta type.

I felt calmer already. The balsam tree in my garden provided shade as well as a place to prep, so I retired to the lounge chair beneath it and blazed up as the sun went down. Kalakuta is excellent for my arthritis, low in THC, and gives a mellow high. And no, I wasn't out of it when I saw them. I'd noticed the tree was loaded with bloated mopane worms, but two stood out. They were abnormally sized, each as large as my torso and radiant indigo instead of the usual dull brown, grey, or green. My jaw dropped.

I pushed out of my chair and pinched out the roach. Then, I dragged the open garden dustbin underneath the creaking branch. The sun was dipping below the horizon when I heard two thumps, and I roused myself to see the enormous worms curled at the bottom of the bin.

My neighbors are from Limpopo, and over the years, I've ignored their kids coming into my garden.

Seasonally, they'd gather hundreds of the caterpillar-like creatures and, after harvesting them, would set to squeezing out their innards. There'd be a green mess of half-digested leaves left, and assorted adults would then smoke, dry, or fry the leftover husks. There was always plenty of accompanying music, dancing, and beer.

I'd always partake and favored the fried version, slathered with a murderously spicy sauce. I learned to love their meaty crunch and to forbear the scalp-prickling and eye-watering that followed. Now, I was torn, wondering what these massive larvae would taste like. Or what they'd pupate into.

The decision of what to do with them was taken out of my hands when the bin started to rock violently. Before I could close the cover, two surreal creatures burst forth. Each trailed a clear goo, and fragments of cracked shells scattered in their wake. They unfurled fragile-looking but massive deep blue, tie-dye-patterned wings. They had full, sensuous lips, were a shiny blue-black all over, and their pupils were oversized and vertical. Both had prominent antennae that poked through their afros and swiveled away from unusually large foreheads.

They were a matched set, each anatomically correct, and had no body image issues, so there was a slight problem with where I could put my eyes. Nevertheless, I tracked them nervously as they flitted all over the garden until they perched in a tree. Fortunately, our homes are setback a fair distance, but I worried as security lighting lit up my new flying friends in a bluish glow, filtered through their wrapped-around wings.

Their lips didn't move, but their antennae did, and I heard a high-pitched chittering with a thick Nigerian accent in my head. They were crestfallen that only regular-sized worms remained but asked me to help find more of their ilk and convinced me with a pretty good party trick; they descended, and hovering above the ground, danced the kpalongo, aka the 'Lagos twerk.'

I felt that dance in my bones.

My eyes were screwed shut on account of their nudity, but I didn't need sight to feel my muscles tighten, the pain from my arthritis recede, and my spine straighten. Plus, praise the Lord; when the one with boobs touched me, there was an unfurling below my belt. With impeccable timing, my doorbell rang, and the creature reacted with a startled shriek. The other one joined in, and I opened my eyes to the ancient nurse screeching at me to wake up.

I was back in that drab airport waiting room. Customs picked me out like a speck of shit from a bridal gown. I should've complied sooner, but now, handcuffs are cold on my wrists, my suitcase's contents are all over the place, and the air is stiff with the smell of Kalakuta. The customs guys waddled out, eyes downcast, most whispering urgently into their phones. Two of them left, hand-in-hand.

They took the weed with them but not the aroma, so when Nurse Toothless came in to do a health check, her nostrils set to twitching. God help me, but my pump was primed already. I felt lift-off. When she locked the door, and her gums set to gumming, I shrugged and closed my eyes.

146

The Regular

Robert Burns

The restaurant was mostly empty. It was a typical Monday evening—a welcome quiet after the bustle of the weekend. The passing, all-day, rain showers had settled into a cold, steady drizzle for the night.

At the stroke of eight, I spied Mr. Johnson entering the outer door of the vestibule. Always dressed neatly in a dark navy suit and colorful tie, he was slight of build, yet distinguished. His skin was the color of fine mahogany, and shocking white hair encircled his bald dome. He has been dining with us nightly for as long as I could remember.

I asked him once why he ate dinner here every night—why he was such a regular. He told me he liked the meatloaf, and I believed him. He always ordered the meatloaf.

Even though I'd waited on him for years, that was the extent of our relationship. Friendly and cordial, yet still with the unspoken boundary between patron and server. I've always prided myself on being a good waiter.

I opened the inner door and greeted him with a

broad smile. "Welcome, Mr. Johnson!"

"Good evening, Willie."

"Your regular table?" I asked, just in case.

"Yes, thank you."

I showed him to the table by the front window and helped him with his overcoat. Handing me his charcoal pork pie hat, the elderly man settled with a quiet wheeze into his seat facing the door.

I hung his coat and hat on the coat tree and presented him with the evening's menu. "What'll it be tonight, sir?"

He perused the specials with a furrowed brow. "I think I'll have the meatloaf."

"Yessir. Excellent choice. Something to drink?" I asked, already knowing the answer to that one too.

"A glass of your finest cabernet, my good man."

"Coming right up."

I put in the dinner order at the service counter and uncorked a fresh bottle of L'Auteur Cellars, a decent red wine, far better than anything else we carried. I always charged Mr. Johnson the house wine price, though. After all, being a regular has its privileges.

I returned to the table with the glass of wine. "Meatloaf's on its way, sir."

"Thank you, Willie."

As was his custom, Mr. Johnson surveyed the street as he sipped his cabernet. Occasionally, he craned his neck to scrutinize some passerby on the sidewalk, eyes twinkling in anticipation as if expecting someone special. Invariably, his eyes sank as disappointment returned to his face, realizing he was, once again, mistaken.

I brought his supper to the table and set the plate carefully in its place.

"Here you go, sir."

"Ah, yes. Smells wonderful," Mr. Johnson said, reveling in the steaming aroma.

I paused. I'm not sure why I picked that particular night to ask, but I guess curiosity finally got the better of me. "Say, Mr. Johnson, do you mind if I ask you a question?"

"Not at all, Willie."

"Well, I see you here every night, staring out the window, and I was wondering, are you waiting for someone? The meatloaf isn't all *that* good."

"I'm waiting on my wife."

"Oh? Does she work downtown?"

"She's late. Coming in on the train. She's been visiting her sister upstate."

"I see," I said politely, not *really* seeing though, my forehead wrinkled. "Well, enjoy your meal, sir. May I get you another glass of wine?"

Marlene, the owner, stood behind the bar, drying a hi-ball glass. She nodded toward the table as I approached, "Meatloaf?"

"Yep. He's waiting for his wife. Her train is late. I didn't even know he was married."

Marlene dropped the glass in the sink, the color

draining from her face. "Willie, Mrs. Johnson died fifteen years ago. Train derailment."

"Seriously?"

"He's been coming here ever since. I thought you knew. You wait on him just about every night."

"I know, but—geez. I never thought—."

Shaken, I perched on the edge of a bar stool and watched the old man across the room through different eyes. I could better appreciate his weariness, his burden, as he ate even more slowly than before. I wanted to go up to him and hug him—tell him I understood—but I didn't.

Finished with his meal, Mr. Johnson rose, pulled on his overcoat, and plucked his hat off the tree. He waved. "Money's on the table, Willie. See you tomorrow."

"Thank you, sir," I called.

The aged man walked slowly through the vestibule and into the damp night.

I followed him to the door and stepped outside, watching after him until he disappeared around the corner.

"See you tomorrow," I whispered into the soft drizzle.

The Story of Us

Teodora Vamvu

A novelist could have written the story of us, had we not wanted to write it ourselves.

In our eyes, the first time they locked, at a table in that restaurant our friends made a reservation for.

On our hands, when they touched as we both reached for the check on the first date. I let you pay.

A novelist could have written our story, had we not written it on our lips the first time we kissed, under the flickering light of a worn-down lamp, a treasure passed down for generations until it no longer resembled a gain, but rather a barely hanging leaf in the family tree.

We wrote our story on the rocks we competed to throw as far as possible in that lake we stumbled across after an agonizing 4-mile hike. You wrote it in your passion for exploring nature, and I in my passion for you.

In the car, as we headed to your parents' home up East; on the Goodyear tires that navigated swiftly down the road, with all its twisting and winding.

I wrote it on a piece of paper I attached to your gift that first Christmas together. You wrote it on the toothbrush you smuggled into my bathroom cup.

We wrote it on the key chains we attached at each of our sets of keys, to the house we decided to move into together.

We wrote it in the earth where we planted our first tulip bulbs. On the wood planks we chose to cover a small part of the garden, so we could sit on chaise lounges and sip lemonade.

We also wrote it on other things.

You wrote it on the walls of our bedroom as they reverberated, riding the wave of your fury as you worked at your most expansive decibel level. The family lamp trembled.

I wrote it on your T-shirts when I accidentally washed them with a pair of hot pink yoga pants. Accidentally.

You wrote it on the inside of your palm as it imprinted on my chin. I wrote it as annotations in the book I threw at your head. You wrote it on the knuckles of your right fist as my stomach twisted and bent under its will.

I wrote it inside the ink of the pen I used to sign the abortion paperwork.

You wrote it in the waiting room, on the chair you never sat on.

I wrote it on the diamond-shaped kitchen tiles on which my tears and blood pooled together, never really blending perfectly, a maelstrom of stupor and despair.

You wrote it on my stunned expression as a brutally forceful pull took me aback. My pained realization as a piece of white cloth made breathing impossible. I wrote it on the single tear that streamed down my face before I closed my eyes and surrendered.

Now I'm scratching the entirety of our story on the insides of the wooden box I awoke in. You are writing it on the dirt and gravel that's making it hard to drag. On the shovel you are most certainly carrying under an armpit.

I can hear the tulips shedding their last petals.

I am writing it on the back and front of my teeth as I grind them together. Because I am also writing it in the screams I don't let out.

The story of us could have been written by a novelist had I not wanted to write it with you.

Raincoat and Tissues

Kerr Pelto

I don my mother's black raincoat, a perfect fit, and leave home.

Rain embraces the cemetery, endeavoring to cleanse it of sorrow as a train's lonely whistle echoes my thoughts. Standing over my mother's grave, I lay newly cut peonies on her headstone. It feels like only yesterday, yet a lifetime ago, that her ashes were interred. Another fall, winter, spring, and summer have slowly passed.

Looking down from the heavens, does my mother know a great-grandson was born? Did she see other grandchildren running around in the rain last week? Can she feel it when I miss her, think of her, speak to her?

Maybe those things don't matter. Perhaps memories of good times spent together in the past give the todays added meaning.

I think of yesterday, when I drove by my mother's favorite stationery store. I remember walking up and down the aisles with her, searching for just the right envelope and paper for her ongoing correspondence.

The emergence of email and social media didn't lessen her love of hand-written letters on beautiful paper.

Someday, I'll enter the store again. I'll slowly peruse each aisle and think of my elegant mother who loved written words. When I find the perfect envelope and piece of paper, I'll return home, sit at the desk she left to me, and write a letter to say "I love you, Mom."

As I turn to leave her grave, tears mingle with raindrops on my cheeks. Unconsciously, I reach into the pocket of the raincoat and find tissues Mom left behind. My laughter, full of joy, tampers my grief. Of course, there would be tissues in my mother's coat pocket! She always carried them with her, just in case.

As I wipe away my tears, I feel my mother *has* seen me here, *has* heard my thoughts, *has* felt my sadness as well as my happiness.

Rainy days will always need a raincoat, tears will always need tissues, and I can always write a hand-written letter to someone I love.

Robert Burns

Robert Burns is a classically trained architect who brings a designer's eye to his fiction. A writer in many genres, his stories have appeared in numerous online publications as well as several print anthologies, including a fantasy story focusing on Novel Characters, a piece of detective fiction, a dystopian Christmas tale, and the first chapter of a historic novel currently in the works. Robert writes full time from his home in Richmond, Virginia.

Readers can also find his work online at his own site, *Robert Burns: Chapter Next.*

Bryn Eliesse

Bryn Eliesse is a writer from the East Coast of the United States. When not drinking tea, you will find her in the literary worlds of romance, fantasy and science fiction. As well as a collection of short stories printed in several anthology books, she has a half-edited novel, a half-blind cat, and a half-baked idea of what to do with her life. Writing is her passion, so whatever the future holds, it will play an integral part.

Ryan Fleming

Ryan Fleming is a Director of Critical Care at a hospital in Birmingham, Alabama, USA. He lives with his wife and two children, who are always eager for a bedtime story. Ryan has been published in anthology books and online. With a challenging work schedule, you can find him on many late nights with his laptop, hot tea, and smooth jazz playing as he works on his current work in progress.

James Hancock

James Hancock is a writer/screenwriter who specialises in bizarre comedy, thriller, horror, sci-fi and twisted fairy tales. He takes readers down strange and seldom trodden paths, often dark, and always with a twist or two along the way. A few of his short screenplays have been made into films, his stories read on podcasts, and he has been published in several print magazines, online, and in anthology books.

He lives in England with his wife, two daughters, and a bunch of pets he insisted his girls could NOT have.

Mikayla Hill

Mikayla Hill is a published writer who dabbles in a variety of genres and formats. From poems to short stories, she enjoys the craft of putting words to a page. She has many notebooks and word documents filled with stories in various stages of completion, from the bizarre and fantastical, to sweet and sappy, to the shockingly twisted.

She lives in the West Coast wilderness of New Zealand with her partner and two sons, and hopes to one day be able to support them with her writing.

Séimí Mac Aindreasa

Séimí Mac Aindreasa, having taken a brief 50-year hiatus from writing, in order to deal with growing up, returned to the field of play with 2023's well received drabble anthology, the Dark of Day, a collaboration between 6 international authors. The anthology book, Bring out the Wicked was his second time in print. Raised in West Belfast, he remains there, looked after by Susan and ruled over by their beautiful children and the dog, who Susan is exasperated by. The dog, not the children. Well, also them, sometimes.

Oluseyi Onabanjo

Oluseyi Onabanjo currently lives in New York City with his wife, as do their two grown children. He qualified as an engineer in the pre-internet age, and still bears the scars. He holds an MBA from Columbia Business School in the City of New York and an MA (with Distinction) in Creative Writing from the University of the Witwatersrand, Johannesburg, South Africa. He has had stories published in the *Potomac Book Review* and *Rock and a Hard Place* magazine. Oluseyi's 85,000-word fantasy novel, which he plans to publish in 2024, is presently fermenting in a dark drawer.

Kerr Pelto

Kerr Pelto is a born-and-raised Southerner from North Carolina. Listen closely; you might hear her accent in her stories. Entering contests feeds her competitive nature, earning her recognition in publications. As a professional calligrapher, she has been a contributing writer for the calligraphic world for decades. Don't let her southern, gentile ways fool you. Her stories bely her Catholic upbringing. She might need to go to confession. Kerr lives with her husband who graciously listens to her tales. Her house is always abuzz with her grown children, grandchildren, and granddogs, not to mention the chickens.

Sarah Turner

Sarah loves to write short fiction and poetry, and her work has appeared in anthology books and publications such as Lucent Dreaming, Writers' Forum, and Writing Magazine. She lives with her partner in England, where she works in education and watches too many quiz shows.

Teodora Vamvu

Teodora Vamvu is an online content manager from Bucharest, Romania. Some of her short stories have been published in anthology books, online, and some are hiding in a folder on her desktop. The rest are here.

When she's not writing, she's reading, and loves books of almost all genres; especially those with a clever twist.

If you enjoyed this book of short stories, please look for others on Amazon by the same authors. Thank you.

Timeless Tales

COPYRIGHT © 2024

Printed in Great Britain
by Amazon

Timeless Tales

Tales of love, loss, horror, suspense, and the bizarre

35 moments in time